HIS

(A Dark Erotic Romance Novel)

By

Aubrey Dark

CHAPTER ONE

Gav

The best part about choosing a victim... well, for me, it's the little things.

Seeing what they do for fun, that's always eye-opening. This one, my next, he was a strange man. He normally went from his job as a university attorney to his home, where he would beat his wife and son and then go to sleep.

He had only one minor deviation in his schedule. Every week or so, on a Saturday, he would stop off at the college library to drop off and pick up a book. A legal thriller. They were always legal thrillers.

Legal thrillers and crime fiction... _bah_. The authors writing that stuff don't know what it's like, or they would write it different. They don't know the pleasure of driving a knife into someone's hand as they cry for mercy, the pleasure of seeing the blood bubble on their lips when their throat is cut.

The pleasure of all the screams: the screaming drowns out the thing that drives me mad. It drives away the shadow.

Yes, I'm sanest when I kill.

Usually, the men I kill are the ones who make sure their own misdeeds go unseen. When they beat their wives, they hit them in the stomach. They would never leave a mark, or society would know.

I don't mind leaving marks. Nobody will see their bodies, anyway. They're cowards, all of them, cowards and bullies that will disappear without a trace.

I climb the library staircase to the second floor, where the genre fiction is kept, thinking about how I will do it even as I watch him climb the stairs above me. His legs move like puppet legs, wooden and mechanical up the steps. Inhuman.

I'll follow him to his car, I think. Then the syringe, the catch.

Then the kill.

Kat

It was a beautiful spring day in California. The arboretum glowed with dappled sunlight and college students wandered lazily through the green paths, enjoying a weekend off from class. In the native sagebrush, orange butterflies danced in the air, and above us, oak leaves glittered silver in the breeze.

I couldn't have cared less.

"Will you hurry up, Jules, *please*?"

"Kat, you have got to be the most boring person I know. Stop and smell the roses! And by that, I mean there's a super cute guy over there painting in the rose garden." Jules tilted her head to one side, her purple-tinted bangs falling over her face. "An artistic guy. I like that."

"We don't have time for guys. We're already late!"

I was shuffling quickly through the arboretum, dragging my coworker behind me through the gardens. All around us, college students wandered lazily around in pairs and groups. A dozen sorority girls had put out a blanket so they could work on their tans on the grassy lawn, and every guy who walked past slowed to half-time to gaze at the rainbow of bikini bottoms covering skinny tan asses. I shoved my way past the ogling meatheads.

"We're only, like, ten minutes late," Jules said, sighing as I yanked her out of the sunny arboretum and through the library doors. We hustled past the front counter to the back, where I grabbed a cart quickly and pretended that I had already started shelving.

"You're *so* lucky Sheryl is late." Our boss was, as Jules put it, more sadistic than Disney's Ursula and less forgiving than Inspector Javert.

"Lucky, nothing. I knew she would be late. You want to skip back out to the arboretum and check out that artsy guy?" Jules gave an exaggerated wink.

"No."

"You're never going to find a date with that attitude."

"I date plenty of guys."

"Sure, Kat. Right."

"I do!" My cheeks flushed as I pushed the library cart full of books to the elevator. Jules followed me, flipping through one of the books that we'd just gotten in.

"Since when do you read romance novels, anyway?" I asked, hoping to change the subject.

"Ugh, never," Jules said, tossing the book back onto

the cart. "Such boring protagonists. The same old plot. Romantic heroes doing romantic gestures. Maybe you should read one, though."

Ha. There was nothing in those bosom-heaving books I found sexy. I would never admit it out loud, but even the new "racier" stuff didn't do much for me. I wanted a hero who would push me to the edge of insanity, a man who would make me *feel*.

"Why would I read, uh, *The Rogue's Hidden Past*?" I asked.

"Let's see," Jules said, pointing to the back cover. "To *find out his terrible, dark secret*."

"I bet it has something to do with kilts. Do you *see* this cover?"

"Those are some sexy manlegs. Manlegs that could be wrapped around your waist."

"Jules!"

"You know why you should read this, Kat? You should read it because it might get you in the mood for some sexing."

"Jules..." I pushed the book cart harder toward the elevator. So much for changing subjects.

"What? Kat, really? You haven't gone on a single date since you started working here."

"That's because I *just* started working here."

"Two months ago," Jules said, rolling her eyes.

"Two months is not a lot of time to meet a guy." God, had it been two months already? I definitely had to get out more. But overtime at the university paid well— *really* well—and I was saving up. "Plus I have to work."

"Work, schmerk. Come out to the bars for once. Isn't it your birthday soon?"

"Maybe."

"Maybe?"

"Yes. Next week." I sighed. I was turning twenty-three, and I was still a junior at college. Well, now not even a junior, unless I could get financial aid. All around me, I saw people a year or two younger than me graduating, getting jobs. And here I was, falling even further behind them. Ugh.

"I can't, Jules. My loans fell through, and if I don't save enough for tuition, I—"

"—won't be able to come back next semester," Jules said, finishing my sentence for me. "You know, you don't have to spend money at a bar. *I'll* buy you a drink. *Guys* will buy you drinks. Especially if it's your birthday."

"I don't want a guy to buy me a drink. They always think that I owe them something afterward."

"You do. Just like you owe me some sex from the last time I covered you for a six-pack."

"Is that an offer? I don't even know how lesbian sex works."

"It would work better than your current sex life. Or lack thereof."

"Oh, man, better call the fire squad, I just got *burned*."

"No, but seriously, I'm ready to do a sex intervention, Kat. A sextervention."

"That's not a word."

"Stop being so boring."

"*Boring?*" My mouth dropped open. "I am not boring!"

Compared to Jules, I *was* boring. If a seventies

punk rock star had sex with a Japanese schoolgirl and had a baby, that baby would be her wardrobe. Her hair was buzzed and spiked except for her long bangs, her tongue was pierced - along with a few other body parts - and her roster of guys—and girls—rotated as quickly as her clothes selection.

"When's the last time you kissed a guy? Or flirted with one?"

"I haven't seen a lot of guys around," I said, shifting my weight from one foot to another. I knew that was an excuse. There were plenty of hot guys around the university. I just didn't want to be rejected again. It seemed like every girl at school was a hot blonde sorority chick, and I was a mousy brown pile of nothing. Even when I put on makeup, it seemed futile.

And there was something more than that. The boys I'd dated... they'd always been vanilla. Maybe it was all of the books I'd read, but I wanted more. I wanted the whips and ties, the spanking, the whole shebang. But I had always been too shy to bring it up except once, and the guy had looked at me like I was crazy.

Maybe I was crazy. Maybe nobody actually did that in real life. I couldn't help but dream of a man who could dominate me the way I really wanted, even if he didn't exist. I shook the dream out my head. I definitely wasn't telling Jules any of that.

"Plus, they would never go for me. I'm not even a student here anymore now."

Jules pushed the elevator button and held out a fist in front of me.

"Look. Do you see this? What is this?" She waved her fist inches from my nose.

"Um. Are you going to punch me?"

"No."

"Are you trying to teach me sign language?"

"No."

"Is this you coming out to me as a member of the Black Panthers?"

Jules opened her fist to show an empty hand.

"This."

"There's nothing there."

"Exactly. This," she said, waving her empty hand around, "is *all the fucks I give* about you not being a student. I don't care. *Nobody* cares. All the guys looking to get laid do not give a single solitary fuck about you not being a student."

"Fine. Fine." Jules may not have had the most eloquent way of getting a point across, but it got there. "You tell me what to do to get a boyfriend, I'll do it."

Jules held the elevator door open for me. I pushed the library cart in. She followed and smashed the elevator button for the third floor with her fist. I winced.

"Okay, look. The next cute guy you meet, you have to kiss."

"*What?!*" My pale skin immediately blushed red hot. "No way."

"Way." Jules raised an eyebrow at me. "You said you would."

"I..." I looked over at my co-worker. She raised a fist, and I knew my pleas would fall on deaf ears. She truly gave no fucks, and she also might punch me.

"Fine," I said, plotting to leave work early so I wouldn't have to get dragged to a bar. If I never saw a cute guy, I wouldn't have to kiss him. Right? Right. My plan would work perfectly.

"Fine?"

"Fine. You know what, fine. I will."

"Good."

"If it'll get you to shut up about my dating life."

"Or lack thereof."

"Or lack thereof," I repeated.

"Excellent," Jules said. "You might escape a life of boring tedium yet."

"And I'll have nobody but you to thank for it."

The elevator jerked to a halt at the second floor and the doors opened. The man standing in front of the elevator doors took a step forward. He was dressed in a crisp white button down shirt and black pants, with dark brown hair and a sharp jawline that hinted at a five o'clock shadow without admitting of stubble.

When he looked up at me, his eyes were like the ocean before a storm. Gray-green slate, calm and confident. I dropped my eyes and saw that the top button of his shirt was opened, his smooth chest peeking out from the fabric. He looked like a model from the cover of the romance novel Jules had just tossed onto the book cart.

He looked like someone who could tie me up, hold me down, fuck me hard and crazy. I blew a low breath through my teeth.

"Welp, this is my stop," Jules said, hopping out of the elevator before I could think about anything other than those eyes. "See you on the third floor!"

Wait. Oh, *shit*. No, I couldn't!

I tried to push the cart out but Jules shoved it back at me. A half dozen books spilled out of the bottom shelf.

"One more floor, Kat!" Jules said, her voice forced and bright. As the man turned and stood next to me, Jules coughed in his direction, her eyes wide as saucers. My mouth dropped open. *No. I couldn't.* I couldn't. Oh god, I couldn't.

Jules raised her fist as the doors closed.

Oh god, I had to.

Gav

The days before a kill are delicious. I savor them. Every minute I spend tracking and following gets me more and more aroused. More hungry.

The thing I crave is a thrill I can only get from another's death. The look on their face when they realize I'm about to end their life. Like a shot of heroin straight to the heart. Not that I do drugs, mind you. I used to, but you grow bored with drugs after a while.

And I've never grown bored of killing.

The shadow drives me out to look for prey, but that's not the real reason I was there. I don't just kill because I need to. I kill because I want to.

I'd prepared almost everything this time for my spring kill. I'd cleaned out the kitchen, gotten everything set up. I had to pick up some new batteries for my alarm system, but that could wait until tomorrow. I still had another week before the man would return to this same library.

I stepped into the elevator and picked up the books the library worker had dropped, setting them back on the cart for her. There was something in the way she looked at me that gave me pause. Did she recognize me? Had she seen me following the steps of the man I was about to kill?

I glanced again out of the corner of my eyes. She was staring at me like she knew I was a killer. Fear beaded on her forehead. I turned to her, and she swallowed.

"I'm sorry," I said politely, consciously relaxing my jaw. "Do I know you?"

"I'm sorry," she replied. "I...I have to do this."

Kat

I threw myself forward, my eyes closed. *God will forgive me*, I thought, *but Jules never will if I don't kiss this guy.*

The man didn't even flinch as I pressed my lips to his. I smelled the subtle touch of his aftershave on his cheeks, and his skin was soft against mine. I expected him to shove me away, to yell at me, to get me fired— *oh, Lord, I hadn't even thought about that!*

I expected, that is, just about any reaction other than the one that actually occurred.

He kissed me back.

As soon as I felt my lips touch his, a spark flashed through my nerves, drawing me close to him. One of his hands gripped my wrist and the other gripped my waist. He wasn't pushing me away, he was simply holding me as though there was nothing strange at all about a girl throwing herself into his arms. His lips pressed back on mine, seizing me, and dizziness seized me, making the walls of the elevator spin as he kissed harder, harder, sucking the breath out of me.

Yes, I've kissed guys before. No, I'm not a virgin. I've dated around, and even had a couple of one-night stands. This, though—this was different. There was a ferocity in his kiss that swept me up completely, a brutal hunger that spoke of a desire no other man had ever revealed. Maybe no other man had ever felt it. Whatever it was, it shocked my entire body so much that I couldn't respond, couldn't do anything but keep kissing him back.

This was what I wanted – the way he held me so completely in control. The way he pushed harder against me, brutally. In that instant, I imagined him taking me wholly, violently, making all of my dark fantasies come true...

Then the elevator stopped and so did he.

As he stepped back, I had to lean on the cart to keep from falling over. Swooning, I guess they would call it in a romance novel. His eyes searched mine, and a chill went through my bones. From up close, I could see his eyes, and they were flat, a green-gray swirl that stopped on the surface. It was like looking into the eyes of a statue: lifeless. Disappointment trickled down at the back of my mind. For me, it had been the best kiss I'd ever had. For him, though, it seemed like nothing at all had happened.

The elevator doors opened, and still I stood there like a dummy. The doors had started to close when his hand shot out to hold them back.

"This is your stop?" he asked.

"I—oh—yes, I—" I stammered. I moved slowly, like I was underwater. One of the library cart wheels got stuck in the elevator gap and I shoved it hard to get it going. It was only when I finally got the cart out of the elevator that I realized what the overall goal of this whole thing had been. I turned around to face him.

"Uh, I—that is, would you like to go out on a date?"

"Sorry," he said, smiling just as politely as before, the skin around his eyes smooth and soft. "I don't date."

With that he let go, and the steel elevator doors closed slowly over his gorgeous face, his flat empty ocean eyes.

Jules came running over from the staircase. My heart was pounding so fast that I thought I was going to have a panic attack.

I pulled out my backup pills from my pocket and swallowed them dry. Panic attacks were no fun, and they definitely weren't fun at work - I was sure Sheryl was already looking for where her assistants had run off to. If I could just breathe normally until the anti-anxiety meds kicked in, I'd be fine.

"Are you okay, Kat?" she asked.

I gulped and pressed my lips together.

"Fine. I'm fine. Totally one hundred percent fine. Just need to calm down a little."

"And? Did you do it?"

I shook my head, blushing hard as I pushed the

library cart into the stacks.

Why did I lie? I don't know, not really. I didn't want to provoke myself into another anxiety attack, that was one thing. Reliving the crazy kiss that had just happened… well, just thinking about it sent me into a dizzy spin. But that wasn't everything.

There was something else that I couldn't talk about, not with Jules. I was sure she'd mock me mercilessly, but I couldn't explain what had come over me and I definitely didn't want to explain to her how he'd kissed me back and sent my heart racing, and my mind down a road of dark, sensual daydreams. And then left me without so much as a phone number.

Anyway, there was no way I would ever date that guy. Apart from the fact that he was way out of my league, he apparently didn't date. And the way he looked at me was... weird.

"No," I said, picking a book up to reshelve it and casting one last glance over at the closed elevator.

"Kat, how could you do this to me? That guy was like, Fabio. You passed up the chance of a lifetime."

I shrugged my shoulders, trying not to give myself away. Lucky for me, I blush at the drop of a hat, so Jules could believe that I was all hot and bothered by nothing more than standing at Fabio's side in an elevator. I knew differently. That kiss was something I wanted to keep a secret. For some reason, I thought that the man with the cold gray-green eyes would feel the same way.

"Guess I am boring after all."

CHAPTER TWO

Gav

I reached the fourth floor and passed by the man I was going to kill later. His cologne was horribly overpowering; I could smell it as I crossed behind him, one aisle of books away. The shadow came with me, urging me on. I pushed it back. Patience. Yes. We would have to be patient. But as I walked down the aisle, I thought that maybe I could kill a week early. He was going through exactly the same motions as he had the week before, and the week before that.

Maybe an early kill. If the parking lot was clear. If I had the opportunity. I smiled, glad that I had thought to bring the syringe with me. I tried to make every tracking as much like the real thing as possible. Preparation. Yes. That's what separated the good killer from the great.

I picked out a book at random and opened it up, holding it in front of me without seeing the words. The man shuffled his feet and stood, indecisive, in front of the shelves.

Pick one, I thought. _You won't get to read it, anyway._

The smell of the book in my hands was an old smell, the smell of paper rotting into dust. Libraries were resting homes for all of the dying books. Dead books, dead authors. Incredible, that characters could live so much longer than the people who wrote them. A character in a book might live forever, as long as there was someone there to read him and remember him.

We, though, are mortal, and I do not expect anyone to remember me.

And certainly, nobody will remember him.

The man took a book from the shelf and I followed carefully, taking the stairs on the opposite side. I didn't want to see the girl again, for she might remember me. The girl who kissed me.

I remembered only her eyes. They were brown and sad. I cannot tell you anything else about her, though. She came and went like any other woman in my life, in and out before I could care enough to remember. My thoughts were only on the syringe in my pocket and the man whose life I would steal away before he harmed the world any more than he already has.

Maybe his wife will remember him, I thought. I smiled. I thought of myself as a kind of assassin, one who worked for free. A pro bono hit man. Charity work, not murder.

We were down the stairs. I followed him to the counter and out the door. He had the book in his hands. He would never get the chance to read it. Poor characters in the book. They would die too, being left unread.

He crossed the parking lot and I followed him, checking around the library. Nobody was there. I could do it tonight, yes. The preparations were nearly done. Why not? I deserved a bit of respite from the shadow.

Sometimes the world makes itself just right. The wind blows a certain way. People walk with puppet strings attached to their limbs, and I feel like the puppet master. That was how he walked, across the parking lot toward the place where I would take him.

I had made up my mind. I would do it tonight, a week early. It was the perfect opportunity, and I would not pass it up.

He was at his car and I was there at my car next to him where I had left it, trunk unlocked. Before he could open the door, I spoke out loud, angrily.

"Did you see who parked on the other side of me? Some *asshole* keyed my car door."

The man raised his eyebrows and came around to my side of the car. He was curious. Perfect.

We're all excited to see destruction, of course. We all want to stare at the damage someone else has caused. I'm just more honest than everyone else. I don't wait for the damage to come to me. I go out and find it.

Oh, the man. Yes. Him. One plunge of the syringe was all it took, and he was already unconscious. It only took a second more to toss him into the trunk. The book went on top of his limp body.

Patience had gone out the window. I was so lucky to have had a clear shot, and the adrenaline that rushes through me when I took it – it was like nothing else.

Excitement pumped through my veins as I got into the car and drove away, the body in my trunk. Tonight I would cut off his abusive hands and carve a knife deep into his skin until the tendons pop. I expected that he would cry. Most of them do. I expected that he would beg for mercy. The shadow would retreat with the sounds of his screams. I would hurt him for myself, and for the people he had hurt. He would beg me to let him live.

And then, later, he would beg to die.

Kat

Jules was right. I was boring as hell. I wrote my phone number down on a scrap of paper and ran downstairs after the guy to give it to him, but I couldn't even bring myself to follow him outside. It looked like he was going to talk to that other guy, the professor with the creepy mustache who always checks out the legal thrillers.

I didn't want to bother him. Bother them. I didn't want to be a bother to anyone.

When I die, they're going to write it on my tombstone:

Here lies Kat, the boringest girl ever and totally chickenshit. At least she didn't bother anybody.

I don't know if you're allowed to swear on gravestones, though.

Sighing, I threw the rest of the audiobooks down into the crate to go out for interlibrary loan. Stupid me. I should have run after him. Even if he said he didn't date. That night I lay in bed and thought about his eyes. Thought if I should have gone after him. I'd never felt that kind of chemistry with any guy before. What if he was my one true love, and this was my one chance to get with him? Okay, maybe that was a bit melodramatic, but still. I started looking at every guy who came through the library doors to see if it was him. He didn't come back.

The next day, I felt somewhat better about not giving him my phone number. What kind of a guy kisses a girl back in an elevator? Even if I did start it, , I told myself that I needed to kiss another guy and get over it. There weren't any cute guys in the library, though, and the only person who got on the elevator with me was a sixty year old professor with white hair tufting out of his freckled ears. I sighed and pushed the cart back into the storage room.

"Still thinking about Fabio?"

"Ugh, Jules, shut up."

"He dropped something up in the stacks yesterday."

"What?"

Jules pulled a folded piece of paper from her pocket and handed it over to me.

"I was just going to throw it away, but you're mooning over this guy hard. Maybe if you see him again, you can give it to him."

I unfolded the slip of paper. It had a few lines of numbers written down on it, a code or something. Next to one of the lines, the word *important* was underlined twice.

"What is this?"

"Beats me. Maybe you can ask him to explain it to you when you see him."

"I'm not going to see him." I'd already resigned myself to not ever finding him again. Okay, yes, I was boring. But I also wasn't about to go chasing a guy who had already told me he didn't date. What kind of guy didn't date? It was the politest brushoff I'd ever gotten.

"If you see him, then you can talk to him again.

How about that?"

"How about you butt out of my beeswax?"

I crumpled the paper and stuffed it into my back pocket.

"Sure, I'll butt out. So you're going to keep it?"

"Shut up."

"Shutting up!" Jules grinned and took the carton of discard books from me. "Shutting up right... now!"

Later I came into the back room to find Jules staring at the television in the break room. With a pile of old textbooks in my arms, I came and stood in front of her.

"Get out of the way!" Jules kicked out with her foot and knocked a textbook off the top of my stack.

"Earth to Jules, we work in a library. What are you doing watching TV?"

"You'll never guess who got murdered," she said.

"The president," I said.

"No."

"Your mom."

"No. Jesus, Kat, that's insensitive. What if my mom *was* murdered?"

"Who, then?" I let the pile of textbooks slump to the table near me and turned to the television screen. If our boss wasn't around, I guess a bit of TV wouldn't hurt.

"That guy that comes in every couple weeks," Jules said, motioning to the screen where a police captain was being interviewed.

"That's really specific."

"The professor who reads the shitty John Grisham knockoffs. You know, the one with the creepy look."

"No way." The screen switched over to a shot of the

man with the mustache. I'd seen him just a few days earlier. He'd been checking out a book. Idly, I wondered if his family would bring back the book to the library.

"Way," Jules said.

"Someone murdered him?"

"Well, he's missing, anyway."

"So he's not murdered."

"Oh, sure, he ran away to Costa Rica and left his wife and kid and six figure job. Yeah, right. Trust me, he was murdered. God, you have such a boring mind."

"I don't think I've ever known anyone who was murdered before."

"Well, now you do," Jules said, turning off the TV just as Sheryl rounded the corner, her face stuck in that perpetually pissed-off look that some bosses have. "And now he's dead. Back to work, slacker."

Gav

I told him not to move when I shaved his mustache off. He moved. Then the tablecloth was bloody. He didn't start to scream until I began to shave a little deeper.

It was beautiful.

The begging, too, that was delicious to hear. It drove the shadow away. The blood spilled and made a mess, but it had to happen. He'd hurt his wife, and now he was being hurt. It made a kind of sense, didn't it? And I did so love to hear him beg.

So many promises, this one.

"Let me go, and I'll give you anything. As much money as you want." His voice was whining, needy.

I gestured around me with my knife.

"You've seen my house," I said. "Do you think I need money?"

"What do you want, then? Please. Please! I'll give you anything."

I couldn't wait to cut out his tongue. Maybe in a few days. I poured water over his face and he drank it, lapped it up greedily like a dog. A thought was nagging me at the back of my head. Something I had forgotten. But no, I hadn't forgotten anything. There were no tracks for anyone to follow.

The young woman at the library, the one who kissed me, came floating into mind. I pushed the thought away. Maybe I would go back and return the book, retrace my tracks, make sure I hadn't missed anything. What could I have missed? Still, the nagging thought at the back of my brain kept itching. The shadow darkened my vision and brought me back to my world, to the dead man who did not know he was dead lying on my kitchen table.

"Please," he continued. "What can I do? What do you want from me?"

"Right now?" I raised my eyebrows. "Right now, I want you to suffer."

"Suff-" his words cut off as I came towards him again with the knife. "No, please. Oh god, please, no!"

"Scream," I whispered, bringing my knife down to his cheek.

He obliged.

CHAPTER THREE

Kat

It was a few days more before the man came back to the library, fifteen minutes before closing. Not the mustache man—Jules was right about that, he was gone for good, probably murdered—but the handsome one. The one I'd kissed. The dark-haired, light-eyed Fabio.

Boring old me stayed away. I didn't want to scare him off. This was the only time he'd been back since the first time I'd seen him, when I'd kissed him. And as strict as Sheryl was about helping library patrons, I thought that I would be more help not scaring him out of the library again with a random kiss.

I stayed in the kids' section and shelved picture books, watching as he went up into the stacks and dreaming about all of the dark, terrible, wonderful things he could do to me if he had me in bed. Then he came back down and started to head out of the library. .

My hand reached back into my jeans pocket. I hadn't done laundry in two weeks, and the slip of paper was still stuffed into my back pocket. I pulled it out and looked at it. Random numbers and letters. But it was something to start a conversation about. I could talk to him.

"Hey, you dropped this last time you were here. So

what's important about this code, anyway?"

I didn't know why I was so hell-bent on talking to him again, anyway. If anyone asked, I would probably tell them it was Jules breaking my balls, calling me boring every two minutes and asking me if I'd ever kiss a boy again. I wasn't boring, dammit!

But the real reason I clocked out early and scooted after him?

I wanted to kiss him again.

I wanted to feel that passion.

I wanted to know if his mind was as dark as mine.

In the parking lot, I saw him get into a silver Kia sedan. A boring car, Jules would say. He was too far away to run after, and I thought about giving up and going back inside. Finishing up the picture books section. He probably didn't need the slip of paper, anyway.

But then I changed my mind. The kids' books could wait. What if the paper I had from him was super important? What if he was a secret agent and the paper I had was a secret code? And—bigger question—*what if he kissed me again?* So I hopped into my black Honda Civic, possibly the only car more boring than a silver Kia, and drove off after him.

I'd seen enough cop shows to know how to tail someone. Stay behind, but not too far behind. Don't let traffic lights get between you. Have a boring car. Check! It also helped that the car between us was full of five college frat boys hanging out the windows and blasting music. If he ever looked in his rearview mirror, all he would see was *Animal House* on wheels.

A rush of excitement went through me as I followed

him. I was off work, and instead of going out to bars, I was chasing a sexy guy who might even be a secret agent! There was no way Jules could call me boring after this. Okay, so he probably wasn't a secret agent. But at least I could pretend he was for now.

I crawled behind him from light to light, and he never noticed me. I supposed that this might be a good career for an average-looking girl with an average-looking figure. Men never noticed me: I would make a great undercover cop. I made a mental note to ask the career counselor about it.

Soon, he turned off of the main street and headed out of town. I lagged behind; there weren't any intersections on this road. He kept driving, and more than once I thought that I was crazy to keep following him.

Why? Why did I keep following?

I don't know, not really. I wanted to see what was hidden in those eyes. I wanted to know what the important code was. I wanted to ask him why he wouldn't date. Or if it was just that he wouldn't date me. There was something mysterious about chasing after a guy I didn't know, and my heart beat faster as I drove, excitement pumping through my veins.

I pulled out my phone and dialed Jules. At least I could let her know where I was, in case this guy *did* turn out to be a secret agent. But the little bars on my screen were gone: no reception out here in the mountains. Frowning, I tossed my phone down on the passenger seat. I would just have to tell her about my adventure later.

His car led me to the outside of town and into the

nearby mountains. I slowed even more. The sun was dipping down below the tops of the mountains and I could see his red taillights clearly as he took the curves around the mountain bends.

What on earth was I doing? I was wasting so much gas driving out here. For a split second I considered turning around, but then his car turned into a long driveway. I drove up to the driveway just as his car went around the curve inside. I parked on the dirt pullout and hopped out.

Maybe I should just leave the slip of paper in his mailbox. The metal gate that barred the driveway was swinging shut slowly. I really shouldn't go running off after him. What would he think of me showing up on his doorstep, with nothing but a stupid scrap of paper with some numbers on it?

But it said *IMPORTANT*.

Just as the gate was about to shut, I darted inside. The metal clanged as the gate locked behind me.

"Seriously, Kat," I said to myself. "What the *hell* are you doing?"

I felt utterly stupid. I had driven all the way out here, and for what? Nothing. I considered my options:

1. Climb back over the fence, go home, and feel like an idiot.

2. Ring the doorbell and... feel like an idiot.

"ARGH!" I pressed my forehead against the metal gate, looking at my car through the bars. This was ridiculous.

"Yes, this is ridiculous, Kat," I told myself. "You wanted to play Nancy Drew, well, here's your goddamn chance. Stop being a boring idiot. Okay? Okay."

With that settled, I turned around and looked up the curving driveway in the middle of the forest. Every step I took put one more butterfly in my stomach I couldn't even see his house from the road. Huge pine trees cut off the view after about fifty feet of road. I swallowed. If he was a secret agent, wouldn't he have some kind of security system? What if I got shot or caught in a trap before I reached the house?

"Shut up and walk, Nancy Drew. He's not a secret agent, and you're not going to get shot."

I walked boldly down the driveway, and when I turned the last curve I couldn't help but gasp.

The house was a gorgeous two-story log cabin, with a giant stone chimney stretching out over the tops of the pines. It was incredible that I hadn't been able to see it from the road, but it was tucked away into the side of the mountain.

"Wow," I said.

It seemed stupid, but I felt like a total badass. I'd followed Fabio all the way up here without getting seen *and* I'd slipped through the gate. No matter what, I could go back to Jules with an interesting story.

I went to the front door, but there was no doorbell. As I raised my hand to knock, I heard something from the back, somebody yelling. Then it stopped.

"Hello?" I said. Nobody answered.

"Okay, Nancy Drew, you know what to do now."

Actually, I knew exactly what NOT to do. Normal, boring Kat would have put the slip of paper on the doormat and ran away. But I was curious, and today I was determined not to let myself get in the way of... myself.

With newfound courage, I crept along the side of the house. There was a light on in a room near the back corner, and I made my way through the side yard landscaping, dodging the rose bushes that were planted under the windows. I reached the lit window and, standing on tiptoe, peeked up over the edge of the windowsill.

What did I expect to see when I peeked into the window? I don't know. Fabio sitting in an armchair, reading a book he'd checked out from the library, maybe. I imagined that he would see me and laugh, invite me in for a drink, put on some music and tell me that he was kidding, that actually he would *love* to date me. We would dance and talk and make love all night.

Instead, what I saw made me scream.

Not scream, exactly. More like a terrified mix between a gasp and a yelp that I tried to stop as soon as it came out of my stupid, stupid mouth. Because when I looked into the window, I saw a room with a single metal table and a man strapped down, *covered* in blood. Standing over him was the handsome man from the library.

My Fabio.

Holding a knife.

It might have been the professor on the table. I didn't know. I didn't *want* to know. As I yelped, my hand slipped and hit the windowpane, and if my half-scream hadn't gotten his attention, the loud clunk sure did. Both of the men turned to look at me. Fabio's dark eyes narrowed to slits, locking on mine. My mouth went dry.

Jesus, it's real. He's not a secret agent. He's the

killer. Holy fuck.

"Help! *Help!*" The man on the table began yelling at the top of his lungs, which made me jump again—I'd thought he was dead. Fabio walked around the table toward the window, still carrying the knife. I stumbled back and fell right on my ass under the window. The rose bushes scratched my arm badly as I fell, but I barely noticed the pain. I was too busy freaking the fuck out. I couldn't go back around to the front - he'd be right there. Oh, shit. *Oh, shit.*

I scrambled to my feet in a panic and ran for the forest in a blind sprint. This wasn't what I'd signed up for. Nancy Drew had walked into the last chapter of a Stephen King novel, and she was getting the hell out of there. Behind me I could hear the door opening. Fuck, fuck, *fuck.*

I pumped my arms and legs, trying to gain speed. I was already into the trees, and I could see ahead of me the driveway curving into view, the metal gate I would have to climb over. I angled slightly toward the driveway. Good. Perfect. A shortcut to the exit.

Just as I was coming out of the treeline onto the driveway, my foot caught a tree root. I stumbled, rolling my ankle and falling to the ground. I gasped in pain as I got up to my knees. Hot agony shot up the side of my leg, but I couldn't stop. I couldn't. My mind screamed: *Go, go, GO!*

I scrambled forward on the driveway, the paved surface hot under my scraped hands.

I struggled to get to my feet but stopped dead in my tracks, half-kneeling in the middle of the driveway. My heart dropped down into my stomach.

Standing right there, right in front of the metal gate, was Fabio, the knife held loosely by his side. I hadn't even heard him come up from behind.

His eyes were so calm that for a split second, I was calm, too. As though nothing was wrong with me trespassing and witnessing a murder. I half-expected Jules to jump out from behind a tree and yell that I'd been pranked. The blood, though, dripping off the point of his knife - that was real. His eyes followed mine to the knife. Then he spread his arms wide and dropped the weapon to the ground. It clattered dully against the driveway.

"Don't be afraid," he said.

Gav

"Don't be afraid," I said.

She didn't trust me. Smart girl.

Taking a slow step back on her injured foot, she turned to run. I sprinted forward, and with a single fell motion caught her arm while I pulled the syringe from my pocket, jabbed the needle into her neck. There wasn't a lot left inside, but I hoped it would be enough.

The batteries. I knew I had forgotten something. The damned alarm system, the most important thing of all. The electronic net that protected me. And I had gone and forgotten the batteries! Stupid spring cleaning!

Her delicate hands—librarian hands, I thought idly—clasped at the syringe, then at my wrists. The sedative was already beginning to work, and her nails scratched me only slightly. Soon she was limp in my arms.

I couldn't believe it. All of the luck in the world, the opportunity of getting to kill early, all of my elation was gone. I cursed my own stupidity. Then I turned back to the task at hand: getting rid of her. My witness.

I lifted her up, her round curves soft and voluptuous against my skin. As I hefted her in my arms, I smelled her shampoo, a soft vanilla scent. It tickled my nerves and aroused me.

Lust, intervening.

Normally, I wouldn't mind an interruption, but her presence raised some questions that I could not possibly ignore. She would be awake again, sooner rather than later, and I would ask her then.

Was it mere chance that she landed here outside of my window? Or was she part of some larger plot, a police investigation, maybe? The forest around me was black and quiet, but snipers could be closing in at any moment. I hoped that if they shot me, it would be in the head.

Calmly, then, accepting whatever fate came to me, I made my way back to the house, carrying her already-stirring body in my arms. No snipers shot me dead. Good. Excellent. Now there was only her to deal with.

The shadow swirled at the base of my consciousness. *You could kill her*, it said.

"No," I whispered to myself. *Not an innocent.*

You could keep her for yourself. Torture her. Keep her as a pet.

She moaned softly and I held her tight to my chest,

feeling strangely protective. The shadow would not have her. Step by step I made my way to the front door, all the while listening to the dark voice that murmured terrible thoughts. There must be another way to deal with this.

Kill her. Take her, then kill her. Take her—

I shut the door behind me, closing out the darkness.

Kat

The world bled into my vision. Dizzy, I raised my head and looked up. I was in a hallway. The front door was right there. I was inside. Inside his house. *Oh, god.*

"Wha... what?" I mumbled. I blinked hard, the dizziness making the floor under me fuzzy and indistinct. It was hard. Wood.

"Who are you?"

I turned my head to see Fabio standing next to me, his knife in his hand. Don't be afraid, he'd said, and then he'd stuck me with something in my neck.

Well, I wasn't afraid. I was fucking *terrified*.

"I'm sorry," I gasped. My hand shook in front of me as I shielded myself with one arm. My other hand was planted on the floor. Another wave of dizziness swept through me. How long had I been out? "I didn't... I didn't see anything!"

"Really? You were running quite fast for someone who didn't see anything."

"I didn't!" I touched my neck and my hand came away with a small smear of blood. It must have been a needle. Something to paralyze me. My mouth was cottony. He leaned toward me and I cringed back. "Please! Please! I didn—"

"Are you with the police?"

I stared in blank terror at the knife he held in his hand. The sharp edge glinted in the dim hallway light. If I told him yes, would he kill me? Or if I told him no? I looked up to his face, trying to make out his features. He didn't... he didn't look angry at all. He looked calm. I swallowed. Maybe it was okay. Maybe I could reason my way out of this.

"Please," I said, trying to speak calmly. "I'm sorry for trespassing—"

Big mistake. The man grabbed me by my hair and pulled me to my feet. I screamed and tried to reach for the door, but he jerked my head back against his chest, raising the knife to my throat.

"Shhh," he said. I stopped mid-scream, my mouth still hanging open. The metal edge of the knife was cold as ice on my throat. If I shifted my weight, it would slice me open as easy as anything. *Ohnononono.*

"I don't want to hurt you," the man said. "But I will if I have to."

"Please, no," I whimpered. "Please—"

"No more talking," the man said. "Just smile and nod for yes, or shake your head for no. Okay?"

I opened my mouth to say okay, then realized my mistake. I pressed my lips together and nodded slightly. The edge of the knife was sharp against my skin.

"One more time, then. Are you with the police?"

I shook my head no.

"Is your car out on the road?"

I nodded yes.

"Is there anybody else out there?"

I hesitated, then shook my head no.

"Does anybody know you're gone?"

What would he do to me? Would he kill me if he knew somebody was out there looking for me? Or the other way around? I didn't know, and I was so scared that I fell back on the truth. I couldn't help the tears running down my face as I shook my head.

No. Nobody knows I'm gone. Nobody knows I'm here. There's nobody coming to save me.

Gav

Spring cleaning was my favorite time of year. Cleaning itself was glorious. The shiny sink, the gleaming floors. The bright windows looking out on the pine trees.

And in spring I allowed myself to kill early, before the shadow crept in on me and began to rot me from the inside out. I had *really* been looking forward to this kill, to getting rid of the shadow. And then she had to pop into my nice clean world and mess everything up.

I knew that I couldn't let her go. That much was certain. But I couldn't kill her either.

I mean, I *could*. Don't get me wrong. I haven't cared about another human since I can remember words. I remember –vividly remember—the sensation of looking up at my mother, the sun behind her hair.

Then—darkness—looking down at her body.

After that, there was no caring anymore. Only numbness.

I could kill this woman; the difficulty comes from all of the attendant complications. Her car, for one. Her cell phone. If she turned out to be a cop. Or even if not, whether she'd told a friend where she was going. Whether she had an accomplice waiting for her at the road. Even as I held the knife to her throat I was checking off all of the things I needed to do.

All of the complications that she had brought to my nice, simple, serene life.

Please don't misunderstand me. I'm as peaceful as Siddhartha, ninety-nine percent of the time. It's only that the shadow builds around the edges like dirt on a glass table. It builds and builds, creeping inward, until it reaches the heart, and then the choice is simple.

I have to destroy or be destroyed. And I've always chosen the former.

Interesting, since I don't have much reason to live. But I figure that neither does anyone else. So who's to say I should be the one to go? I have to admit I tilt the odds in my favor when I weigh my lives against those of my victims. It's easy to look through public records. Easy to find the rich men who have settled their abuse cases with fines instead of jailtime. It's so easy to pick out the men who, like me, are capable of hurting others.

They've all been men. I've never captured a woman. Or killed one.

She might be the first.

Kat

"Alright," the man said. The pressure of the knife eased up off of my neck. "Let's go inside."

He let go of me and gestured down the wood-paneled hallway. I choked back my sobs and took a step forward. My leg gave out under me as pain shot upward from my ankle and I bent over, clutching my leg.

"*Ahh*," I gasped. It was almost completely dark in the front hallway, and I couldn't see the features of the man anymore. I didn't know whether he would cut my throat right then and there if I spoke, but I didn't know what else to do. I couldn't walk. I could feel myself beginning to have a panic attack. My pills. Where were my pills?

"It—it hurts," I whispered.

"To walk?"

"I rolled my ankle." The man gave a deep sigh. The knife twirled in his hand.

"Wait! I can crawl," I said quickly. "Please. I'll crawl. I'll—"

"Come on," the man said, reaching out to me. He pulled me to my feet and put one arm around my waist, holding me up. "I really don't have time for this."

I leaned on him and limped down the hallway. All the while, he held me tight against his body. It was terrible to think about, but it had been a long time since anyone had been so close to me, and the way that his hand wrapped around my hip... well, I couldn't help what my body decided to respond to. The pressure of his arm around me was thrilling, in the most terrifying kind of way. I bit my lip as a new wave of pain shot through my leg.

We reached the end of the front hallway and turned into the main living room. I gazed into the house, expecting to see gleaming rows of torture weapons. Knives littering the floor. A bathtub full of body parts.

Instead, I saw a living room right out of the center page of Home & Living magazine, a log cabin that any millionaire might have owned. A leather couch in front of a huge fireplace. Brass radiators on the walls. Plush velvety rugs on top of knotted pine flooring. And, through the open door to the kitchen, a table where a man lay, bloody and groaning.

Okay, maybe that scene wasn't in Home & Living.

He stopped at the end of the hallway in front of a closet and slid open the pine door. Inside of what I'd thought was a coat closet stood a rack of computer screens, showing every possible angle of the house and the surrounding property. The road, the gate. Three of the screens had a red blinking icon at the top that said *Warning: Intruder* in big block letters.

He frowned and pulled out what looked like a remote control. He opened up the back and tapped the remote. Four batteries fell out.

"Goddammit." His voice was flat, but there was so much anger simmering under the surface that it might have been better had he yelled. He ripped open a fresh back of batteries with his teeth and replaced them, then tossed the remote control into the closet and slammed the door. Turning to me, I saw irritation written all over his face.

"Out of battery," he said. "My audio alarm is out of battery. That's why it didn't go off for you. Great.

Spring cleaning and I forgot to change the batteries."

My mouth dropped open. That was it? If he'd changed a battery, I wouldn't have witnessed a murder? Well, almost a murder, I reminded myself, as the man in the other room groaned again.

"If you let me go, I won't say anything," I said, my words rushing out in a flood of worry. "I didn't see anything. I don't know your name or who you are. I don't even know who that guy is!"

"Why are you here?"

He stood facing me, his flat eyes accusing me. I gulped.

"I... I was curious. About the paper."

He stepped forward so that our faces were only inches away from each other. I smelled him again, the subtle aftershave mixed now with sweat from his exertions. There was another smell, too, underneath all that. The smell of blood, coppery and bitter.

In spite of everything, I remembered the last time we'd been so close together, in the elevator. I remembered his fierce kiss, the passion that swelled up and tore my breath from my lungs. Even standing so close to him now, I felt the same terrible desire come racing through my body, turning me hot between the thighs. I knew he was dangerous, but my body didn't care.

"Curious. You seem like a curious one."

He looked at me like nobody else had ever done before. I was used to guys giving me a quick once-over, their eyes sweeping across my face and down my body in a blink. His eyes, though, caressed the lines of my face with a penetrating gaze that I could almost feel on my skin. He reached out and touched my chin, and I flinched at the touch, thinking of blood.

"Like a curious little kitten."

His hand moved down trailing over the seams of my clothing. He touched my waistband, sliding his fingers around the back, over my pockets. He stopped and slid his hand into my back pocket. I held my breath, but he simply pulled out my car keys and put them in his own pocket. In my other jeans pocket he found the slip of paper.

"There it is," I said.

"What? This?" He unfolded it and glanced down at the numbers. "Is this some sort of code?"

"That's what I was curious about," I said. My heart was pounding. Was he working for the government? Maybe he was a trained killer. Then there was no way he could kill me. I clung to that small bit of hope. "What does it mean?"

But he only raised his eyebrows.

"How should I know what it means? Looks like a bunch of random numbers to me."

"It's not... it's not yours?"

Fabio shook his head slowly, peering at me as though I was the crazy one.

"But my friend told me—"

I cut myself off as I realized exactly what had happened.

Jules!

What did she say? *Maybe you can ask him to explain it to you.* Holy shit. She faked it. She faked a stupid secret note so that I would talk to him again. And it worked, better than she could ever have imagined.

Or worse than she ever could have imagined.

Jules, you have no idea what you've done to me.

"A mistake, perhaps?"

"My friend..." I choked on the words. "She wanted me to talk to you."

"That makes more sense," the man said, relief coming over his face. "Yes, more sense than you being with the police. Here I was thinking that they might be onto me! But no, it's only... it's only you."

The man finished patting me down and then took my arm.

"Look what you've caught, kitten," he said, smiling. "Come here."

His arm came around my waist again and I walked with him for a few steps before realizing that he was taking me to the kitchen. The man inside on the table moaned.

"No," I cried. "I don't want to see—"

"Too bad, little kitten," he said, pulling me along with him. I stopped walking at the doorway but he was too strong: he simply dragged me the rest of the way. He pulled me inside and dropped me next to the radiator in the corner before rummaging through a kitchen drawer. I clutched my bad leg and stared at the man on the table.

It was the professor; I could see him clearly now that I was close. There were straps holding him down at the neck and arms and ankles. His shirt had been sliced open and he had three long cuts running up and down his chest from his bellybutton to his collarbone. He moaned again and then opened his eyes. His mustache was gone, shaved off.

He had dark brown eyes, eyes like prey. They found

me in the corner, and he twisted his head, as shocked as I was that I was here. He opened his mouth, and blood ran down his bottom lip.

"*Run*," he said hoarsely.

A new wash of fear swept through me, and I would have run if I had a leg to do it with. But before I could do anything, Fabio stepped over and grabbed my wrist. He snapped a handcuff on me and snapped the other half of the handcuff onto the radiator.

"What are you—"

"I'm glad you're so curious, little kitten," he said. He went back to the man on the table and shoved a dishcloth into his mouth just as he began to scream. The screams turned to muffled chokes as he pressed his hand over the dishcloth to hold it in place. "You'll get to see everything much better from inside, I promise. It's almost confession time. And we have a lot to confess, don't we?"

He picked up the knife from the table and drew it up along the edge of the mustache man's jawline. The man's muffled scream turned to a high pitch, and I watched in horror. The handsome man lifted the knife up into the air.

He smiled. Dear god, he smiled.

CHAPTER FOUR

Gav

There's something about killing that soothes me. And after such a harrowing night, I needed to be soothed.

I took the knife and slid it down to the man's chest. He was bawling behind the dishrag. Behind me, the girl was crying, her eyes clenched shut. Stupid girl. She told me she was curious.

Licking my lips, I took my time. My favorite is the skin on the chest, when it opens up in nice thick slices. Almost like bacon.

I'm not like Hannibal Lector, don't worry. Human flesh doesn't interest me, not in a culinary way. I do enjoy watching people realize that they are all flesh, though. It's something I've always known about myself, but most other humans have the mistaken idea that they're _people_, not just animals. They think that there's something separate from their bodies, something different and disconnected from the tissues and tendons that take them from place to place in the world.

They're no different, though, when they start to die. Like this man, for instance. I slipped my knife under his skin and he howled behind the dishrag. Blood welled up from under my knife and dripped down his side. In the corner, the girl was speaking.

"Don't do it, please don't do it," she said. "Please, don't hurt him anymore."

"Shut up," I said, not looking at her. I still had to decide what to do with her, but I didn't want a distraction. Not now. "You have no idea how much he deserves this."

My knife sliced down the man's chest, down to his stomach. His screams softened the edges of the world. He sounded so much like an animal now, so very much. I took out the dishrag and his howls filled the room.

The girl clapped her hands over her ears. Silly girl. This was the sound of living. This was suffering at its purest. It was beautiful, really. Justice for the innocent. Pain to pay for the pain he had caused.

The howls increased as I tapped the knife's edge on the man's hand, just at his knuckle. He balled his hands into fists.

"How did you hurt her?" I whispered to the man. The point of my knife pushed down into the first knuckle of his index finger.

"No," the man gasped. "No."

"I didn't ask if, I asked how," I said calmly. The man's eyes sought mine, but there was nothing in them but fear. He was an animal now, and the only thing he cared about was surviving. "Did you hit her?"

"No!"

My knife punctured the skin and I drove the point into the knuckle.

"I saw you," I said, my voice a sing-song. It wouldn't be long now. He would confess. "I saw you."

"No—"

I twisted the knife and the bone popped. The man's

scream brightened the room.

"I saw you." The calm came over me. It would be soon. The world brightened with color already. "I saw you."

"I'm sorry, I'm sorry, please don't, I'll never do it again, please, no, no, no—"

The girl in the corner was crying, her face buried in her arms. I was sorry that she had to miss this. I looked into the man's eyes. When I first caught him, he was arrogant. His eyes were full of hate and power, and he thought he could get away with hurting people. Now all there was in his eyes was hurt and pain and terror.

A monster for a monster. Something to feed the shadow.

The fear of death was a powerful emotion. It dropped away everything else and cleansed people of their sins. Nobody, not even the cruelest man, can hold onto their cruelty in the face of death. It takes away their power, makes them humble. It was a blessing to them, I thought, that they died in such purity. And it was this purity that fought away the shadow inside of me.

"You can't get away this time," I said to the man. He had stopped pleading—all that came from his throat were whimpering sobs. Beautiful, beautiful. The world was bright again. He was ready for death. I was ready, too.

"Kitten," I said, placing the tip of my knife at the base of the creature's throat. "Look here. Look here, kitten."

The girl raised her head, and I plunged the knife deep.

Kat

I closed my eyes but I could still hear the man dying. His throat gurgled with liquid, and then silence.

Tears ran hot down my cheeks.

"I don't want to be here. I don't want to be here."

I thought maybe if I said it enough times, it would be true. I could click my ruby slippers together and teleport back to the library, where Jules would convince me that I should shelve another section for her. I would be back in my boring life, doing boring things in a boring place. I'd be *safe*.

Then I opened my eyes and saw the blood puddling on the floor under the table. I was a long way from home.

The man had gotten out an electric saw, and I turned away as he lowered the saw to the body, sending a spray of blood over the front of his shirt. My stomach heaved and I gagged, dry retches that scratched my throat. *No. I'm not seeing this. No.*

I closed my eyes. My palms pressed hard against my ears but the sick buzzing noise still came through. My head was bent against the radiator, and my body curled up into as small of a ball as I could. I didn't want to see this. I didn't want to hear this.

Finally the noise stopped.

The noise stopped, but my eyes were still clenched shut. I heard him walk back and forth, and when I opened my eyes again the body was gone. He wiped up all of the counters and the tiles on the floor with paper towels and dishrags. The white terrycloth bloomed red as he cleaned, and the scent coming from the spray bottle he used was the smell of bleach.

I dropped my hands away from my ears. I didn't know what to do. There was no way to escape, and now I'd just witnessed an actual murder. There was no chance in hell he'd let me go now, not after what I'd seen. I felt dead inside, numb. My stomach churned and I didn't care.

Panic attack? I was beyond having a panic attack. I was struggling to even think a single coherent thought.

The killer came back into the room and finished cleaning up a few stray places where there was blood. Then he began to unbutton his shirt.

"What are you doing?" The words came out of my mouth before I could reach out and snatch them back out of the air. Great, Kat. Way to get the serial killer to remember you're still there.

"Cleaning up," the man said, as nonchalantly as if I'd asked him while he was washing dishes.

He took off his shirt and tossed it on the middle of the bloodstained tablecloth.

Then he unzipped his pants. I swallowed hard as he stepped out of the black suit pants and added them to the pile of clothes on top of the table. His hair was dark at the roots with sweat, and his muscles gleamed with moisture. If hadn't been utterly terrified, I would have enjoyed watching him take off his clothes. He was built like a Greek statue, not a single ounce of body fat. Of course, he wouldn't be fat. Serial killers couldn't be fat, could they? Oh, lord, I was going insane.

He stripped off his socks, bending over. His back was taut with heavy muscle, and I felt sick thinking about how I had wanted him, how I had kissed him. He pulled off his underwear last, throwing it on top of the pile.

Oh my god. Oh shit. He was going to rape me. He was going to rape me and kill me and take me apart. I couldn't help but stare at his naked body as he moved, folding the tablecloth on top of the clothes. He wasn't aroused. Not yet. Maybe he would only get aroused after cutting me like he had cut that man.

Hot tears burned my eyes. Why had I insisted on breaking my boring routine? I could be studying in bed right now, instead of waiting to have my throat slit by a murderer.

He gathered up the tablecloth and left the room.

I heard him moving in the living room, and then the sound of the fire crackling. He was burning everything. His clothes, the tablecloth, the body. Everything. Even now I could smell the charred scent of what I realized was burning flesh. It would have turned my stomach, but my stomach was already turned.

The kitchen was clean, now. It looked like a normal kitchen. I stared at the place where the body had been. Fifteen minutes ago, there was a person lying there. Now... he was gone. A queasy shiver went through my body.

That would be me. He would take me and use me and cut me to pieces. My breath began to come quickly. Panic attack. No, Kat. Don't panic. You can't panic, or else you'll never be able to fight back. I struggled to relax as the tension clenched my chest tight.

He walked back through the door, completely naked, and looked at me. He frowned. It wasn't an angry frown. He looked at me like I was an object, not a person. Like I was a bag of trash he'd forgotten to take out.

"Well," he said. "That's done. Time to deal with you."

He stepped forward and I screamed.

I wasn't about to go without a fight. Sure, I didn't have any weapons, and this guy seemed strong enough to break my neck with a single twist. But I wasn't going to let him rape me and kill me without giving him a couple of scratches. I got to my feet, hunched over the radiator for support.

He stepped forward again and I kicked out with my foot. The blow glanced off of his leg and I kicked again, but this time pain shot up my other leg. I gasped in agony, bent halfway over. He cocked his head, looking confused.

"Don't you touch me," I said. "Don't...don't you hurt me."

"Why would you think I would hurt you?"

I stared at him, my jaw dropped open.

"I—you—you just killed that guy!"

"Yes? He needed to be killed. And?"

"Well... and..."

I stammered for breath. What was going on here? It was like some sort of crazy nightmare where nothing made sense. The man leaned on the kitchen counter and rubbed his temple with two fingers.

"What exactly are you worried about?" he asked.

"You!"

"Me? What do you think I'm going to do?" He moved forward again quickly, and before I could raise my leg to kick him he'd stepped on my foot, pinning my one good leg down. I raised my fist but he caught it easily and wrenched my arm up over my head. I panted for breath, expecting at any moment a knife to be slashed through my throat.

"Tell me, kitten," he said, his voice a purr. "What exactly are you worried that I'll do?"

"Kill me," I whispered. "Torture me. Rape me."

"Rape you?" He chuckled. I couldn't believe it. I'd just watched him stab someone to death, and he was laughing at me for being afraid of him. He truly was insane.

"You're naked!" I cried out. He stepped back, letting go of me, and looked down.

"True. Well, I had to clean up," he said. "Would you like me to put on some clothes?"

I stared at him. I had no idea what was going through his head. I was just relieved that he wasn't planning on raping me.

"No?" He reached over and unlocked the handcuff from the radiator, holding it like a leash. "Well, let's get you to the basement then."

Gav

I took her down to the basement, holding her tightly as we walked down the steps. She limped, but I wasn't going to trust her. She'd kicked out at me before, and playing injured was something every prey animal did.

"Don't do anything stupid," I said. "There's not

much here that can be used as a weapon, except maybe the wine bottles." I nodded over to where my cellar collection stood. "And if you try that, I'll just bring a gun with me and shoot you. They're expensive vintages," I added.

Her head nodded slowly. She stood in the middle of the basement, her arms crossed over her chest, tightly hugging herself. Despite her tear-stained cheeks, she was quite beautiful. It was a shame she'd followed me home. Shame I'd forgotten to change the batteries.

I flicked the light switch.

"The light's here. I'll bring a blanket for you. And food, later."

I went to leave and her voice piped up. It sounded thin in the empty basement.

"What are you going to do with me?" she asked. Her lip quivered.

"I haven't figured that out quite yet," I said, and shut the door.

CHAPTER FIVE

Kat

After he left, I scoured the basement for anything I could possibly use to escape. A few empty paint cans were all that lay on the ground near the door. I pissed in one. No way was I asking him if I could use his bathroom. He'd probably want to watch, the creep.

There was nothing in the corners, nothing behind the rack of wine but a stack of cardboard boxes so heavy I couldn't pull them out. I could probably break one of the wine bottles and use it as a weapon, but I believed him when he said he'd have a gun.

No, fighting him wouldn't work. There weren't any other doors in the basement. I didn't know how I could escape. I was beginning to hyperventilate. I sat down in the middle of the basement and hugged my legs to my chest.

Well, Kat, I told myself, there's nothing you can do right now. But it doesn't seem like he's going to kill you, not yet, anyway.

How could I get him to let me go? It was impossible. I thought of Jules working in the library. What would happen tomorrow morning? She would get to work and I wouldn't be there. I was never late. She would realize something was wrong. But how would she know what had happened? She wouldn't.

Terror took hold of me again and I let myself sob.

Let it all out, Kat. Let it out. Cry and be done crying. Then I could figure something out. It was better than letting myself go into a full-fledged panic attack, anyway.

I must have sat there for an hour before he returned. His hair was wet and dripping, but he was wearing clothes. He had brought a blanket. He put the blanket on the floor.

"I took care of your car," he said.

I looked up at him, unsure what he meant. He raised his hand and mimed driving a car off of a cliff.

"Down in the canyon. Sorry about that, but you won't have any use for it here anyway."

I breathed in sharply. I'd saved for two years to buy that stupid car, and despite the more pressing situation at hand it still hurt me to think about my car being destroyed by this maniac.

"My car..."

"I'm sorry, I truly am. Same with your cell phone. It would be stupid for me to keep them around, though. And I'm not a stupid person." He looked at me as though hoping for agreement. "Your wallet was in there, too. Kat, is it? I think I'll keep calling you kitten. Curiosity killed the cat, you know."

"Please," I said. I could hear my voice trembling no matter how I tried to steady it. "Please, I won't say anything if you let me go."

"See, now that would be stupid," he said matter-of-factly. He pulled up the extra chair and sat on it, setting the blanket to the side. "And what did I just say about being stupid?"

"You're not a stupid person," I whispered.

"I'm not stupid," he said, nodding.

"What are you going to do with me?"

"For now? I'm going to keep you here."

I began to cry again. I didn't want to, I didn't want to make him mad, but I couldn't help it.

"No," I said. "Please don't. I don't want to stay here."

He spread his hands out in front of him.

"There's nothing I can do."

"I'll run away," I said, choking on my sobs. "I'll escape and run away."

He frowned.

"Now that would be very stupid," he said. "Very stupid, indeed."

"I'll scream," I said. Anger was building up inside of me and I couldn't keep it from pouring out, just like I couldn't keep myself from crying.

"Then scream. Do you know how far we are from anybody else out here? Go ahead, try. It won't work."

"Please," I said, desperation creeping through my chest. "Please let me go."

He shook his head.

"The sooner you realize that you're here for good, the better," he said.

He stood up and I scrambled to my feet, limping after him.

"No, please. Please don't leave me here. Please!"

He kept walking to the door. I grabbed his arm and he whipped me around in a single motion, pinning me to the wall with his own body. I hadn't realized how tall he was, but he had me lifted inches off of the ground. My toes scraped the floor just barely, and my hurt ankle screamed with pain.

He spoke, and I could feel his hot breath on my face. His dark eyes sparked and he moved one hand over my hair, brushing through it with his fingers. I had fucked up. I had played with fire, and now it was going to burn me.

"Do you really want me to stay down here with you?" he whispered.

I cringed. His body was pressed against mine, and in spite of everything I could feel myself responding to his touch. He shifted his weight and pushed one of his legs between my thighs. I burned with the pressing ache there.

"You wanted me before, in the elevator," he said, his eyes searching mine. "Do you want me now?"

A shiver ran down my spine. My lips parted, but all I could do was shake my head slightly from side to side.

"No? Then stop tempting me."

He stepped back and let me down. I fell to the floor, clutching my hurt ankle. He flicked off the light and the room went dark, but I could still see his silhouette in the doorway, looking back at me.

"Have a good night," he said, and shut the door.

Gav

The girl had given me an idea.

No, not to rape her. I get no pleasure out of harming

innocent people. Harming guilty people, on the other hand... that was a delicious prospect to drive away the shadow. But not her.

There's really only one thing I could do, if I didn't want to kill her. I could convince her to stay. It would be hard, I know. She seemed different than most of the people I've met out there in the world. I'm not sure how. Perhaps it was simply that she'd thrown herself at me the first time we'd met, and the timing was right. Her kiss had woken up a little part of brightness in the world, if only for a second or two.

If I wanted her to live, then I had to break her. To make her think that she would be better off here, where I kept her in chains. I would have to make her love me. It was the only chance I had to keep myself from killing her.

Kat

The morning light came through the window.
Window.

I sat up suddenly. The room I was in was dark except for the single small window. Where was I?

Then I remembered. The man on the table. The blood. The knife. All of the sleepiness evaporated in a wave of terror. I was being kept hostage in a basement. He was keeping me here.

But there was a window.

I got up, feeling my ankle ache under the weight of

my body. I didn't know how badly I'd hurt it, but I knew it wasn't good. Shifting my weight onto it, I thought I could at least walk. Not run, but walk. It was getting better.

Looking around in the dim basement, I saw the empty paint cans. I'd have to stand on them to reach the window, but I doubted they were heavy enough to break through unless I really had leverage to swing at the glass. I tiptoed over to the cans and set them down underneath the window, then stood on top of them. I could just reach the ledge.

It was one of those small cellar windows, so dirty that I couldn't see anything out of it. All I could see was that there was sunlight coming through, so there must be an opening. If I could get out there, I could run down to the road. I could—

But that would come later. Right now, I needed to get *out*. The window was big enough for me to crawl through, but just barely. And there was no way I was trying to escape out the front door, not with a killer waiting for me with a knife.

A water pipe ran down from the ceiling to the floor of the basement right next to the small window. I pushed my foot against it and it held fast. I could use it as leverage to climb up. Perfect.

First, I tried to push the window open. There wasn't any lock that I could see, so I shoved my hand against the window pane, hoping it would force it outward. No luck. I braced my good leg against the paint can and tried to push. The paint can tilted with the pressure under my feet, and I lost my balance. I fell and banged my knee against the wall, holding onto the window ledge with both hands. My breath rushed out of me in a painful gasp.

Okay, so that wasn't a good plan.

I needed to break the window pane. There was nothing down here heavy enough, though. Nothing but...

My head twisted toward the wine bottles. They would certainly be heavy enough to break the window, I thought. I picked one off of the lower rack and hefted it in my hand. He would hear the noise. But by that time, I would hopefully be out of there.

I stood on the paint cans, my breath coming fast. I would have one chance. I'd have to get through as quickly as possible. I took a deep breath, lifted the wine bottle, and swung.

CRASH!

Glass shards from the window came shattering down over my head. I swung the bottle again and the rest of the pane broke through. Sunlight poured through the broken window, and I could see the forest beyond. I grabbed the edge of the sill and tried desperately to pull myself up. My feet slipped against the water pipe but didn't hold.

Oh, god. I wasn't going to be able to make it. Last semester Jules had signed us up for a rock climbing class as an elective. I had gone once and never again, and now I was regretting it. My arms were just too weak to hold my weight.

No. I had to do it. A noise from upstairs made my heart jump into my throat. Footsteps. *Oh no!*

I crouched down and jumped up as high as I could, clutching at the broken pane. My hand caught on a glass shard and a stabbing pain went through my arm. Blood welled on my skin. I ignored the pain and pulled hard, hard—

"What in the—"

The voice in the doorway behind me made me pull harder. The light in the room flicked on.

No!

My feet kicked at the pipe, scrabbling for purchase. I had my elbow on the ledge, pulling to get through, when I felt an arm come around my waist and hold me tight. Glass tore at my shoulder.

"NO! NO!" I was so close. So close! Blood poured from my arm as I reached out. I had my hand in the dirt outside, but the man was pulling me back in. My fingers clawed at the windowsill, but it was no use. Blood ran down my fingers, made them slippery. I had no hold on the window. He dragged me back inside.

"No! NO! Let me go!"

I flailed in his arms, trying to punch him in the head. He caught my arms and held me in a bear hug, pressing me against his body. No matter how I twisted, I couldn't get out. My eyes couldn't stop looking out towards the sunlight, toward freedom. Would I ever get to see the sun again? Or would he kill me now, here, in the dirty basement?

"You're—Jesus, you're cut badly," he said. His grasp loosened. Now was my chance. I took all of my energy and whipped my head around, smashing it into his nose.

He let me go. Go! I ran to the basement door and limped up the stairs. Blood flowed down my arm, but I pushed myself to keep going. I could make it, and if I didn't then I would die. Die trying to escape. I was halfway across the living room when I felt his hand grab my shoulder. I turned to swing at him again, but then I felt the pinch of a needle in my neck.

Heat washed through me and the room spun. I saw him draw back, the syringe in his hand. Then I fell backwards and the world went black.

CHAPTER SIX

__Gav__

Stitch by stitch, I sewed her arm shut. I did not want her dead, no, not if I could help it. I wasn't that much of a monster, and there was something in her face that made me want to know more about her. I could always kill her later if I decided I needed to, anyway.

The glass had sliced through the lower part of her arm, almost to the bone. She was lucky it hadn't severed the artery. Lucky, too, that I was there.

I'm sure she wouldn't think so.

Was it luck, then, that brought her to me? Dumb, blind chance that set her outside my window? No, I thought there was something more to it than that. Even though I was an abomination in every sense of the word, sinful beyond normal sin, I couldn't believe in a world that was so cold and unthoughtful. There had to be something behind this girl, this beautiful girl appearing at my doorstep.

The devil planted temptation. Dare I pluck this flower?

I pulled the needle through her skin.

Not for the first time, I wondered what it would be like if I were squeamish about blood. So many people were, after all. It was a normal fear.

I had always loved bodies, the sheer corporeality of

their flesh, the hard bone tied together with thick knotted tendons, the sticky tissues.

And her body…

She was asleep and didn't feel anything, but I still felt a strange nervousness when I ran my hands over the curves of her living breathing person. Her hips rounded into thick thighs, ripe and smooth. Her chest moved in slight gasps of breath. Inhale, exhale. Her hands, pale and delicate, her fingers cut sensibly, her wrists—

Her wrists.

I leaned closer to her body, smelling her scent. Turning her palm up, I ran my hand over hers and stretched out the skin along her wrist.

Scars, running alongside the carpal tunnel. White dimpled lines from a knife's edge.

I knew those kinds of scars. Old scars. I knew all kinds of scars. But these scars were attached to a body I found myself much intrigued by, and I could not let go of her hand once I saw them. My fingers traced the line of those white subtle seams over and over again, as though trying to stroke the truth of it out of her body.

"Tell me, kitten," I whispered, although she could not hear me, *"why did you try to kill yourself?"*

Kat

When I woke up again, I was lying on a hard surface. I tried to lift my head, but there was something holding me back. I twisted my head and glanced down.

There was a strap holding down my wrist. And my neck. Straps against my bare skin.

I was on the kitchen table. Wearing only a bra and panties. He'd taken off the rest of my clothes.

"Awake?"

I screamed. The man stood up over me, his face looking upside down at mine. I was trapped. Oh Jesus, I was tied down. I screamed again, whimpering sobs of a scream that came out in spasms.

He waited until I was done screaming, and then he bent down lower. The strap around my neck tightened, then went slack. I lifted my head.

He cupped his hand around the back of my neck, holding my head up. His hand was strong around my neck, and the tips of his fingers grazed my throat.

"Your arm was cut badly," he said. "It needed sutures."

I looked down to see my arm bandaged up. Red blossoms of blood flowered at the top of the bandage. I tilted my head back, settling back into his palm.

"You stuck me with the syringe again."

"I didn't think you'd let me stitch you up if you were conscious. You seemed much too eager to bleed to death while escaping."

"How did you know how to do the stitches?" I asked. My breaths were quick and shallow. I looked into his eyes. I wanted to see if he would torture me, kill me. I wanted to ask him questions forever to keep him from remembering that I would be better off dead and cut up and burned in the fireplace.

"I used to be a medical student," he said. "I was going to be a doctor."

Questions. More questions. Anything to keep him talking, to keep him from getting angry.

"Why'd you stop?"

He smiled and his eyes went blank, as though focusing on something in the far off distance.

"I tried, I really did. I loved working with the human body. They're such remarkable things, bodies. So perfectly made to survive. I would have loved the academic work, certainly. But that whole thing about first do no harm? Doesn't quite work with my personality."

"What *is* your personality?"

His eyes refocused on mine, and I saw them narrow.

"You know my personality, kitten," he said. "I have a taste for killing."

"If that's all you are, then why'd you save me?"

"You have a lot of questions, little kitten," he said. His hand began to knead my neck. My lips parted as his fingers dug deep, massaging the tense muscles. "So many questions."

I gasped as he brought his other hand up to my shoulder and began to rub. The motions were automatic, clinical. But as he worked his fingers into my skin, I could feel my body relaxing. He knelt down at the table behind me so that I couldn't see his face. All I could sense were his hands on my neck, his strong, possessive grasp so close to my throat that I could hardly breathe.

"I have some questions for you, kitten," he whispered. His breath was hot on my ear, and I trembled at the low growl of his words. One of his hands left the back of my neck and moved around to the front. His fingers were long and taut, and they slid down my side, rubbing my skin in slow circles.

I couldn't help it. The touch of a man's hands all over me made me sigh, and at that sigh he nuzzled the top of my head. A terrifying mixture of desire and disgust swept through me. Then his lips touched my hairline just above my ear, and he spoke again.

"First I would ask you why you kissed me," he said. His hand slid down under my bra, and I drew a sharp breath as he cupped my breast. "Did you think I was handsome? Your prince charming, come to take you away on horseback?"

I didn't answer right away. What would I say? But his hand never stopped massaging the back of my neck, even when his other hand squeezed my breast softly. I whimpered as his fingers came up and took hold of my quickly stiffening nipple. Then he pinched me hard, twisting, and I cried out, arching my back against the table.

"Tell me, kitten," he said. He released my nipple, his fingertips stroking it gently. Then he pinched hard again, so hard that I saw white flashes behind my eyelids.

"Yes!" I said, breathless. "Yes, I did! It was a bet! I'm sorry!"

"A bet?" He came to the side of the table, my nipple twisted in his fingers. His eyes were flat, dull green stones that burned all the more with their indifference.

Then he reached down between my legs. I froze. His fingertips grazed the fabric of my panties and my mouth went dry. He was touching me there, right there, and I could barely feel the sensation. A slight stroke up, then down. Up. Then down. His hand moved as though he was idly feeling the top of a tablecloth and he never looked down, not once.

The small voice hiding away inside of me began to crackle and whisper. *This is what you want*, the voice said.

No. Not what I had in mind when I thought about a guy tying me down. Not this.

Then why are you aroused?

I'm not. Not...

This is what you need.

I breathed shallowly, watching his every move. His other hand still held my nipple tight, the ache there beginning to throb through my stomach. He did not watch my body: his eyes were fixed on mine.

"Tell me about this bet."

"Please—"

"Tell me." His thumb rubbed my nipple, rolling it hard. I moaned. He eased off and his other hand stroked me through the fabric, so gently that my body arched to meet him before I pulled myself away. My core clutched itself with repulsive need, and I felt myself grow wet. I threw my head to one side, closing my eyes. No. I didn't want him. Didn't need him.

Maybe if I told him everything he would leave me alone. Maybe he would see how harmless I was, let me go.

The small voice said: *maybe he'll give you what you want.*

I gulped air and spoke.

"It was stupid. My friend said I should kiss the first attractive guy I saw. And—

"And you saw me."

"Yes."

"And you thought I was attractive?" He pushed harder.

"Yes," I moaned.

"What was it that attracted you?" His fingers split apart, stroking both sides of me through my panties, but not the middle. Not where I ached. The fabric was soaked through and I ached, god, I ached so badly.

"I don't—I don't—"

"Tell me. What was it about me?"

"You looked…" My heart was pounding. I needed release. It was horrific to be so aroused with nothing to do about it. My arms were pinned back and I twisted under the straps, trying to get out.

"Yes?"

I breathed in deeply. I had to answer. My mind cast back to that day, a week ago.

"You looked… lonely. Like you needed someone to make things better."

He paused, and the ache that swept through me at the pause took away my breath. *Touch me*, I wanted to cry out. *Don't stop.* I bit my lip hard.

"Kitten," he said. "You might understand me, a little bit. But I didn't need to kiss someone to make things better. I kill people to make things better. Bad people."

He smiled and ice ran through my veins.

"And now I'm not lonely either. I have *you.*"

With those words, he rested my head back down onto the table and left me in the kitchen, still aching for release that he would not give me.

__*Gav*__

She was a complication, indeed. My head swam with it even though I hadn't had a single sip of brandy that day. She kaleidoscoped my world. *And I had just finished spring cleaning!*

I left as soon as I found myself beginning to respond to her body. Attraction is a dangerous thing. I couldn't risk falling for anyone, not even one with a body as lush as hers. It disappointed me that she tried to escape. She cut her body up so badly.

Not as badly as before, I thought, thinking about the small white seams along her wrists.

But no. I needed to train her to behave. Not to run away. To stay inside properly. She could be my pet, the little kitten. And once she learned to behave, then... *maybe*. Maybe I could chance something.

Not yet, though. I run the risk of overlooking something, like the window. There will be many ways to escape, and she would be looking for all of them. And it would be a terrible thing to have to kill her.

Ah, my kitten. Your curiosity infected me.

I'm human, certainly. I can breed with other humans, and my offspring would be human. I'm just not a *person*.

There's no emotion behind anything that I do. This curiosity was a new thing.

In my line of work, I've seen many bodies. Fat, thin, muscled, scrawny. Many of them have scars. A seam along their stomach from a gastric bypass surgery. White marks on the knees from childhood bicycle accidents. I thought that nothing about a body could make me feel anything at all. It's just flesh, just cells. But the scars on her wrists would not go away. When I closed my eyes, I saw them.

That night I stayed up staring at the ceiling. My finger drew a line down my wrist, tracing the path she must have carved with a knife. I shuddered.

Who could do such a horrible thing?

CHAPTER SEVEN

Kat

An hour passed, maybe two, before he came back to the kitchen. I'd calmed down a bit. There was no way he would have stitched up a cut before murdering me, right? At least, that made sense in my mind. If I could keep him placated, I could figure out a way to get out, even if it took a while. Even if he did... _other_ things to me. I shuddered at the twist of unwelcome desire that ran through me at the thought.

When he walked in with his knife gleaming, though, I couldn't help but cringe.

"Easy, kitten," he said. He opened the fridge and pulled out a plate of something, but I couldn't see what it was. Oh, lord, I hoped it wasn't human parts.

I swallowed and tried to relax. Questions. Get him comfortable.

"My name is Kat," I said. "What's your name?"

"Your name is kitten, kitten. Why do you want to know my name?" His back was turned to me, silverware clanking against a plate.

"I want to know more about you." I said, gulping.

He peered at me over his shoulder, his brows suspicious.

"A name means nothing. You can call me Gav."

"Gav." I cast around in my brain for more to keep

him talking. "Is that short for Gavin?"

"Gavriel," he said. "My parents were religious. At least, my mother was."

He turned back around with the plate and I saw it clearly now. No human parts - a rotisserie chicken, mashed potatoes and some green beans. He put the plate down next to my head. I could smell the meaty scent of the chicken and it reminded me of the smell of the man he'd burned in the fireplace. My stomach wrenched and I tried not to heave.

A loud clang brought my attention back to the table next to me. He'd set the knife down right next to my cheek.

"Wha—what's that?"

"Dinner," Gav said. He forked a mouthful of chicken into his mouth.

"I mean the knife."

"It's a knife, kitten. It's nothing. Just a prop. If I'm going to be a serial killer, I have to have a knife." He chuckled.

"You *are* a serial killer. What do you mean, just a prop?"

"Just a prop. Like Chekhov's knife." His jaw worked, chewing the next piece of meat, and I frowned.

"You mean Chekhov's gun."

"Oh, no," Gav said. "I don't believe in guns. Here." He put a fork of chicken under my nose. "Have something to eat."

My stomach growled. Even with the terrible reminder of the smell of meat, I was hungry. I hadn't eaten since... well, since lunch the day before. Reluctantly, I opened my mouth. His eyes tracked my lips and did not leave them even as I chewed the cold chicken. My appetite came back with a crash after the first bite.

"Why not?" I asked after swallowing.

"Why not what?"

"Why don't you believe in guns?" I asked. He offered another fork of food and I took it.

"If you shoot someone from far enough away, you can't even tell that they're dying. You won't even get to see them die. You don't get to see what you've done. It's sterile, bland. It's not a kill if it's not up close. You miss all the good parts."

I nearly choked on the bite of food, but managed to force it down.

He continued to feed me, small bites of mashed potato and beans and chicken. Cold leftovers, but I had never tasted anything so delicious. Even as his words made me shiver, his actions told me that he wouldn't kill me. No, he would do worse. But maybe I could escape.

He sighed, looking off as I finished the bite.

"Guns make death inhuman," he said.

"Would you call yourself human?" I asked, a thin line of bitterness running into my voice.

"Of course I'm human. Human is a species. I'm not humane, that's all. I'm not a *person*." His eyes seemed to change colors as he talked, grayish shades of green and blue that swirled around on the surface but never admitted any deeper.

"Then what are you?"

He shrugged.

"A persona. A character on the page, comprising as many dimensions as the edge of a knife. I kill, that's all.

That's what I am. A knife."

"Nothing else?"

I wanted to see behind the mask he was wearing. I was sure there was more to him, something that I could take from him. Something I could use to guilt him, seduce him. *Something.*

"What do you want me to say, kitten?"

"I don't know. Something. Anything. Or have you just always been a serial killer?"

"I've been many things. A doctor, a healer."

I coughed on the bite of food, and he chuckled at my reaction.

"Yes, a healer. Now, though, I don't just sew up wounds. I stop the wounds before they start."

"You kill bad men."

I tried to make it seem like I understood. I wasn't sure if it was working. He sighed.

"I suppose you could say that. I make them suffer. I take away their sins."

"It must be hard."

"Which part? The kidnapping part, or the torture part, or—"

"Afterwards."

"After I kill them?"

"Aren't you... don't you feel bad? Guilty?"

"I don't feel much of anything, kitten. I suppose you don't know much about that. There's something in me, a shadow. It dulls everything, makes the world black and white. I don't feel guilty, or bad, or good, not once the shadow is there. I feel..."

"Numb?"

His eyes lifted to mine, and I saw a hurt in them

that immediately vanished. It was as though he'd opened up a bit to me, peeked through the door, and then slammed it shut.

"Something like that."

A tiny plop of mashed potato fell from the fork, down my chin. It landed on my chest, soft and warm against my bare skin. His hand moved down, and I thought of how he had touched me before. The memory stirred something in my body that I tried not to think about.

He wiped up the mashed potato with a single finger, strong and hard against the skin of my collarbone. Then he lifted the finger to my lips.

"Finish," he said.

I didn't dare disobey. I tilted my head forward and sucked at his finger, licked off the mashed potato. His eyelashes fluttered as my tongue touched his skin and there was a softening around the corners of his eyes, but he had no other reaction. I swallowed.

"Gavriel?"

His eyes went cold again when I said his name.

"Yes?"

"What are you going to do with me?"

The calmness with which he smiled back at me only made the answer creepier.

"Are you done with dinner? Yes? Then you're going back down into the basement."

He tucked the knife in his back pocket before releasing my straps. Before I could move, he had his arm around my waist and was helping me off of the table.

"How's the ankle?" he asked.

"Better," I answered truthfully. The pain was still

there, but it wasn't shooting through my leg any more when I put pressure on it. It was still nice to have someone to lean on as we made our way to the basement stairs. I limped down the steps and into the middle of the basement with him half-carrying me.

The window was covered with wooden boards screwed in on all sides. He let me go and I leaned one hand against the wall.

Gav reached out and clicked a handcuff around my wrist. I jerked my arm back, but he had already locked the other cuff onto the water pipe next to the window.

"What?" I looked down at my wrist dumbly.

"That's so you don't try any other stupid escapes. My alarm system is up again, remember? I'll know you're out before you can go two steps. So don't try, little kitten. Even if you manage to get out, it would be suicide."

He opened his mouth as though he was going to say something else, then closed it. A hot rage clutched at my chest. I stammered. He couldn't do this. It was bad enough, being held captive in a basement. Now I was handcuffed to a pipe?

"Please, no." I stepped toward him but the handcuffs held me back. "I promise I won't try to escape. I promise. Please don't handcuff me."

"Should have thought about that before, kitten."

"Please. What if the basement floods? What if there's a fire?"

"Then I expect you'll die. Don't pull too hard on that pipe. Wouldn't want a flood."

Anger choked my throat. He'd fed me, helped me. Strangely enough, I felt betrayed. I don't know what I had expected from him, but he had managed to make me think that he might have some feelings for me. But now he was leashing me up like a pet. My mouth was dry, but I wasn't about to ask him for water. He'd probably set a bowl on the ground for me to drink out of.

He tossed the blanket at my feet and turned to leave. A thought popped into my mind.

"Gavriel?"

"What is it?"

"You said you don't believe in guns."

"That's right." His silhouette was dark against the light coming from the top of the stairs.

"But you told me before that you had a gun. You said you'd come down and shoot me if I tried anything."

"I lied."

"Y—you can't lie!" I blurted.

"Of course I can," he said, and even though I couldn't see his face I knew that he was smiling. "Haven't you ever heard of an unreliable narrator?"

He closed the door and left me. My eyes still blinked, as though if I tried hard enough, I could see something in all of the darkness around me.

Gav

That afternoon I went to the bar on the outskirts of town not far from where I lived. It was where I sometimes went to pick up women. Yes, I do that too. I'm a normal person, really, except for the killing bit.

The shadow that hugs me so tight I can't breathe.

Numb. That was a good word, numb. That's how it felt when the shadow closed in.

But I had killed not long ago, and the craving was satisfied. The world was bright again, and I could see. My kitten was locked away tightly.

On the television I watched the news coverage. After an hour spent sipping beers, I saw the first mention of the case. My kitten's photograph came up on the screen, and I looked down at the rest of the bar. Nobody cared. Nobody watched. Nobody knew the pretty young thing who had been abducted.

There was no mention on the news about her parents. No family at all. Nothing but a college friend, a girl with more piercings than I normally gave my victims, tearful and begging for any news about my kitten. She looked familiar, somehow.

With a snap of recognition I recoiled from the bar counter.

She'd been working at the library. She'd seen me.

My heart began to beat faster and I lifted my beer to my lips to hide my discomfort.

"Another one?" the bartender asked.

"No," I said, throwing a twenty dollar bill on the counter. "I'm done."

I hoped I wasn't done for. I would have to learn more about her. Learn what she was all about, why her parents weren't on the news begging for her to be found.

So many secrets, my kitten had. Almost as many as me.

Kat

Hours passed. It's hard to describe how terrifying the darkness was. Dressed only in my underwear, I shivered, acutely vulnerable to every imagined horror in the corners of the black room. Every so often I'd feel a bug crawl over my foot, and I'd shake it away from me with a shudder. Cockroaches? Centipedes? I didn't know, I couldn't see, and that only made it worse.

Once, a bug touched my hand, and I jerked back instinctively, wrenching my wrist in the handcuff. The metal cut my hand, only slightly, but I could feel the blood slippery on my wrist, tickling as it dried. The bandages on my hands from the glass cuts began to unravel, and I tried unsuccessfully to keep them wrapped around my palms.

I didn't know what time it was, whether it was day or night. The sedative he'd given me made my brain fuzzy, even as it was wearing off. The basement was completely, totally black and I had long stopped trying to slip out of the handcuff. I cried for a while, but that did nothing at all to help and only dehydrated me.

I needed something to drink. I hadn't had anything when he'd fed me, and my throat was parched. My tongue stuck to the top of my palate when I touched it there, sticky with dryness. I closed my eyes and dreamed of waterfalls, of rainclouds.

Water. Oh, god, what I would do for just a drop. The gurgle of the water pipe next to my head taunted me, and I pulled at the pipe before realizing that there was no way I could break the thick metal.

"AHHHHHHHH!"

I screamed, and my throat hurt even worse, tight and dry. Only a few hours ago, I had told myself that I wouldn't ask him for anything. Funny how things change so quickly.

For a while I didn't hear anything. He might not be home.

Then a light came on outside the door, the thin light shining at the doorjamb. Steps came thudding down the stairs outside of the basement.

Gav. Would he punish me for yelling? He'd said he didn't have a gun, but still I imagined him getting sick of me, raising a pistol to my head, pulling the trigger. I would have gulped, but I had no moisture left in my mouth to swallow.

The door swung open, blindingly bright, his figure dark in the doorway.

"I'm back, kitten," he said calmly, as though he was a husband coming home from work. The coolness of his voice made me sick. "Have you been screaming this whole time?"

"Water," I croaked. My tongue pressed against the top of my mouth, trying to wet itself. "Please. I don't have anything to drink."

He came forward near me. His features focused themselves as my eyes adjusted to the light. He didn't look angry. That was good. He crouched down next to me and looked into my face, his expression almost gentle. Had he really gone out for a few hours and left me here? Then there was hope that I could escape, sometime when he was out…

"Oh, kitten. An oversight, surely," he purred. His hand reached out to the handcuff and I offered it to him, hoping that he would unlock it. Instead, he shook his head, his fingers sliding over my hurt wrist.

"Kitten, have you been trying to escape?"

"No!" The word came out of me louder than I'd thought, and the scratchiness in my throat threw me into a coughing fit. "No, I—I—there was a bug, I pulled away and it—it hurt. I didn't, I swear, I swear..."

I left off, the cough taking me over again. His fingers ran lightly down my arm.

"A bug? My goodness, bugs. Scary things, aren't they?" Amusement danced in his eyes as he looked at me.

"Please. Water."

"Oh, yes. Water. You want water. Excellent. Then we'll have to do a trade."

A trade? My heart clenched tight in my chest. What kind of trade would he offer? What could I possibly offer? I didn't have any money, and the only thing of value I owned - my car - was apparently at the bottom of a canyon, thanks to the crazed murderer in front of me.

"What do you want?" I whispered, my throat aching. "Please, I don't have money—"

"No money," he said, brushing my hair back with his fingers to look at me. His eyes locked onto mine and I tried hard not to look away. In the dim light, his pupils had grown into pools of black that threatened to swallow his irises.

"Perhaps a kiss?" he asked.

That was it? A kiss? I nodded quickly. There was no more willpower in me left to argue. If that was all he wanted, then let him. My lips were chapped with dryness, anyway.

"Okay," I said. "Okay, and then—"

"And one more thing," he said.

"What else?"

"I would like you to tell me about your parents."

A sharp breath made my throat hurt even worse, but I couldn't help it. *My parents?* I couldn't—I didn't want to—

"I—I don't—what do you care about my parents?" I stammered.

"I would like to know the basic facts about them," Gav said, pulling back and examining my face. "I want to know their names. I want to know where they live."

"Why do you want to know that?" I asked.

"That's not part of the agreement," Gav said. "The trade is for water only. I need information."

"But, I— are you going to hurt them?"

"No," he said flatly. "Or yes. Does it matter what I say?"

My mom's face flashed into focus in my mind, the last time I saw her. A bruise that ran yellow and blue from her left eye down her cheek. She'd begged me not to tell anyone. I hadn't told. I was a coward. I'd left instead, left her. It was better, I had thought. I thought that maybe my dad would stop if I left. I couldn't hurt her again. I couldn't hurt her now.

"I don't want you to hurt my mom," I whispered. "I can't... please..."

"Tell me their names."

"I can't."

"You won't," he corrected.

"I can't!" My throat burned for water. "Please, please. Just a sip. Not my mom. I can't do that to her.

Please don't—"

He stood up, a frown creasing his face, and turned to leave.

"No!" I cried out. "Please don't leave me. I'll die without water!"

He went away, up the steps, leaving the door open.

"Please!" I screamed hoarsely, my words jagged in the chilly air. He did not respond, and on the steps his shadow grew smaller and then disappeared.

I waited, my eyes fixed on the stairs just outside of the basement. He had told me that he wouldn't kill me, but I didn't believe a word he said. Why would he want to know about my parents?

When he came back, I cringed against the wall. But in his hand was a bottle of water. My whole body ached for that clear liquid, but I was too scared to reach out for it. He paused, right in front of me, and then uncapped the bottle. He took a drink and I nearly cried to watch him gulp down the water.

"So you know, kitten, it's not poison." He held the bottle of water out in front of him. "Stand up. Drink."

I clambered to my feet and grasped the bottle of water in my free hand. Clumsily I lifted the bottle to my mouth.

I'd thought I would be slow and careful not to waste a drop, but as soon as the cool liquid hit my tongue I gulped down the water without any regard, not taking a breath until it was all gone. My stomach nearly retched from the intake of so much water, and I bent over, leaning against the wall until the urge passed.

Oh sweet liquid! I hadn't thought water could taste so good. Whenever I used to exercise, I'd relied on

Gatorade and juice to keep me hydrated, although I knew that they were empty calories. Water had always seemed so boring. Not now, though. Now it was the most delicious nectar of the gods. I tipped the bottle up once more to get the last drops from the bottom.

"Done?" he said, smiling. I nodded. My body, now satisfied that it had drunk its share, began to growl with hunger.

"Food comes later," he said. "Maybe once you've told me about your parents. Or maybe I'll have to find that out myself. But now—"

He stepped forward and grasped my chin, tilting it up. One breath was all I could take, and then I was plunged into a kiss that smothered me.

Oh Lord, his lips. My body reacted in only one way to that kiss, and it was not the reaction I would have chosen, had I been able to choose. I'd thought that I could pretend to kiss him back, but as he pressed against me I found myself unexpectedly pressing back, needing more from his kiss than I thought I had wanted. The dark room around us receded, and I floated in his strong arms.

Then his hand came down along my side, and my consciousness was jerked back suddenly to the touch of his hand on my bare skin. I jerked back.

"You said a kiss. Only a kiss," I protested.

He turned to the door, and I thought he would leave, but instead he swung the door shut. We were submerged in darkness, the only light the one thin slit coming from the stairs.

I breathed hard as he stepped forward, his body blocking the light. When his hand reached out to touch my hip, I grabbed it with my one free hand.

"You said—"

His hand took mine and twisted it up over my head suddenly. His body slammed against mine, pinning me to the wall. His cheek was pressed against my temple, his mouth at my ear. I could feel every bit of his strength, and my entire body was immobilized under his.

"Kitten, you never answered my question," he whispered.

In the dark his lips moved, kissed my temple. His one hand still held me back, and now the other one came running along my bare side, brushing against my shoulder, my arm, my breast. A deep shiver ran through me.

"I'd say you owe me more than a kiss," he said. He shifted his weight and I felt his leg shove between my thighs, pressing against me down there. I gasped at the shock of pleasure that coursed unexpectedly through me.

He kissed my neck, his teeth grazing my skin only slightly. I twisted under his grasp but every movement from me only made his hold stronger, more permanent. And the motion of my legs only caused him to press harder. When his head bent to lick between my breasts, I strained back on tiptoe.

Another mistake. He took advantage of the position to push up harder, lifting me so that all of my weight was resting on his thigh between my two legs. The sudden pressure made me whimper, my body clutching into itself hard.

"Do you like this, kitten?" he asked. The words whispered in the darkness seemed to surround me.

My feet kicked out but my toes only scraped the floor slightly, and the rocking motion sent my body into a hard shudder. God damn him, the ache of pleasure there!

"Please…" I choked as he eased in slightly, sending another ripple of pleasure through my body. My hips bucked forward instinctively and I struggled to control myself.

His hand caressed my hip. Then his fingers went lower, cupping the curve of my ass underneath my panties. He kneaded my muscles there, and I couldn't help it.

"Ohhhhhh," I groaned.

"It sounds like you like this, kitten," Gav said. "It sounds like you *want* this. This is the best way, isn't it? In the darkness. You can pretend I'm anyone at all. Pretend I'm the hero in a romance novel. Pretend I'm the cute guy in your math class—"

"No—" I started to say, but another push from him sent my body into a hard shudder, his hand still kneading the spot where my ass met the back of my thighs. Oh, God, but it felt good! My protest trailed off into another whimper.

"You were so eager for another kiss," he said. I bit my lip and shook my head, but in the darkness I knew he couldn't see.

"So eager to give in again," he said. His fingers slipped farther in and I tensed up, then relaxed as his knuckles dug deep into my muscle there, his fingertips almost touching me where I most wanted it.

"Already so wet. So *wanting.*"

I moaned as he pushed again, and then his lips found mine and I couldn't help it, God, I couldn't help it. I arched against him as he kissed me breathless, rocking, wanting the pressure, needing it—

Then it was gone. He broke the kiss and stepped away so abruptly that I would have fallen to the floor had he not held my up by my arms. My legs wobbled underneath me, my entire body melted with the desire for something that he'd taken away in an instant.

"No—" I croaked.

"No? You want more, kitten?"

A sob choked my throat. It was true, I wanted more. My body would not let me deny the sharp thrills of desire that he drew forward in me. And yet, my mind recoiled from the horror of this man, of everything he was. I shook my head and could not speak.

"I have to go now, little kitten," he said. His hand caressed my cheek in the darkness and I flinched at his cool touch, the touch of a lover. "I'll be back soon, and then maybe we can do another trade. Another bottle of water, another kiss. Maybe another question. Would you like that?"

He didn't wait for me to answer. Instead, he let me go and I slumped to the ground on the dirty blanket. I drew the blanket around my shoulders and cried, not caring how many tears I wasted. I cried in self-pity. I cried for myself, for my mother who I had tried to forget and for all of the time I had wasted out in the world.

And I cried, too, because I wanted him and did not want to want him. The memory of his kiss played again and again in my mind and made me ache so badly. So badly that I touched myself and orgasmed immediately, coming hard against my hand in the dark dirty room. Stifling my moan against the blanket, I tried desperately to forget him, forget his touch, forget how much I had wanted him.

Who was worse? Was it him, the monster, the killer, the freak? Or me, who could not help but desire him despite all his darkness?

CHAPTER EIGHT

__Gav__

It started out as manipulation, kissing her. But her moan made something inside me shiver. It scared me, as much as anything could scare me. That she could have seen what she had seen... and still desire me.

It was the reaction I'd wanted, so why was I so disturbed by it?

Trying to get out of my own head, I went to the library to look up news about my kitten, to see how much information about her disappearance was floating around out in the world.

No, not *her* library, I wasn't that stupid. A local branch, far away from the university.

Despite my otherwise opulent house, I kept all kinds of technology far away from me. No television. No computer, save for the security system. No phone. It made things simple. It kept me safe from being tracked in any way. And it made it easy for me to leave my victims in the house without worrying about them finding a way to contact anyone outside.

Now, I searched for my kitten's real name and came up with a slew of news stories. To my surprise, only some of them were from the past week. I scanned the most recent ones and made sure that the police hadn't gotten any new information from that friend of hers.

Even as I went through the motions, a bubble of curiosity was floating up inside of my brain.

Nothing. There was nothing incriminating me. Nothing even to indicate that the police investigation was treating the case as an abduction. *Missing girl. No further information.* I licked my lips. The fear was already seeping out of my muscles.

Perfect. No push for a large investigation. I'd thought that a missing girl would be a thousand times more interesting than the missing businessmen and lawyers I normally killed. I suppose that my kitten was just lucky.

Or maybe there was more to it than that.

I went back to the older entries. The first headline sent an almost erotic thrill down my body:

Missing Teenage Girl Found

A local teenage girl thought to have been kidnapped was discovered last week...

No wonder no one actually cared.

She'd run away at fifteen years old, it seemed. I scanned through the rest of the article. No mention of her suicide attempt. Maybe it had been later, or maybe they'd managed to keep it out of the paper.

The other articles gave up some small pieces of information. Her parents' names, their hometown. So much for her refusing to give me that information.

My kitten had managed to keep her parents from finding her for over three weeks. She'd apparently filed to claim independence from her parents once she'd been caught.

"Kitten," I murmured as I paged through the text, "why did you run away from home?"

Another question to find the answer to. But at least I knew that I was safe, and with this information, I was even safer. The pieces clicked together in my mind like a puzzle of armor keeping me safe.

She'd run away once... she could have run away again.

_____*Kat*_____

He left me alone again, and I slept, goosebumps chilling me as I clutched the blanket over my shoulders. I didn't know how long had passed, but when I awoke my bladder was full to bursting and I was hungry again and thirsty, though not as thirsty as before. I sat up in the darkness. He'd come for me before when I screamed. Maybe it would work again.

"Gav? Hello?"

A pause. No sound from above.

"*GAV!*" I yelled louder.

The light came on outside the door and I heard his footsteps on the stairs. Suddenly I wasn't sure if I wanted him to come down. The last time he'd come to help me, he'd wanted a trade. I hated asking for more - I was scared of what he would demand in return.

The door opened, and I steeled myself. He wasn't wearing a shirt, and his chest was broad, blocking out the light.

"Yes, kitten?"

"I need to use the bathroom," I said. "And I... I need some clothes. Please. It's cold down here."

"You need a lot of things," he said. He came closer, and I shivered. Because of the cold, or because of him? I couldn't tell.

"What do you have to give me?" he asked.

"I won't tell you my parents' names," I said. I'd decided that I couldn't give in. Not for a bathroom, not for clothes or food or water.

"No matter," he said. "I already have them. And their address."

My mind went blank.

"How—how…"

"A lot of information on public record, you know. And your birthday— my, that's soon, isn't it?"

"Yes," I whispered.

That's right. My birthday was in two days. I'd forgotten. Tears welled in my eyes. I'd planned to go out with Jules and get trashed, dance until dawn and celebrate my hangover with an omelet at Manny's diner. I wouldn't be celebrating anything now. And my mother—

"You'll be twenty-three," Gav said, pacing slowly in front of me. "That's a bit old for a college student, isn't it? Or are you a grad student?"

"No," I said, blushing even in the dark.

"Again, no matter. Schooling is overrated. I haven't used my medical degree in years. Well, I suppose I've used it a bit. Helps to know a tibia from a scapula when you're pulling limbs off of people. But med school was overkill. I might have done as well learning how to be a butcher."

I thought of the professor on the table, the saw coated in blood.

"Don't hurt my parents," I said. "I'll do whatever you ask."

"Yes, you will. You'll do whatever I ask regardless. But don't worry, I have no need to kill. Not for a while, anyway."

"Then why did you ask about them?"

"Ah, kitten!" He bent down, crouching. "I was curious. Like you were curious, kitten."

I closed my eyes. I had been curious. Too curious.

"It smells down here," he said, wrinkling his nose.

"Please," I said. "I'm dirty. I've been pissing in paint cans. I can't..."

I trailed off. He tilted his head.

"I wondered why you hadn't asked to use the bathroom."

He reached forward, and I flinched, but he only unlocked the handcuff from around my wrist. He offered a hand.

"Come upstairs. Use the bathroom."

I looked up at him suspiciously. What was this, a trick?

"Do I need to threaten you to do this? Come on."

I stood shakily. My hands were both bandaged from the cuts, but he took my arm and helped me up the stairs.

The light upstairs was so bright it made my eyes swell with tears. I wiped them away clumsily with my hand. We walked slowly through the living room, then up a set of stairs. He didn't try to rush me, only held me gently with one hand. I suppose he knew that he could kill me easily if I tried anything.

I peeked over once at him. He had a blank expression on his face. His chest was smooth all the way down to his bellybutton, and then a patch of dark hair led down beyond the top of his pants. I bit my lip and looked away.

There was a lot to look at. This place was a mansion. Everywhere I looked, opulent furniture filled the rooms and expensive-looking oil paintings with gold leaf frames decorated the walls. At the top of the stairs, a crystal statue of a four galloping horses greeted us. Their manes shimmered like glass.

"This isn't the end, kitten. Keep moving."

I couldn't keep the wonder out of my voice.

"How do you have all this *stuff*?"

Gav chuckled.

"One man I brought here tried to bribe me. He had a few million wired to my anonymous bank account. Ended up being very helpful. Right through here."

I headed down the hallway he'd gestured to, leaning on him a little more than I had to.

"Did you still kill him?" I asked.

"Of course. He'd seen my face."

I stopped mid-stride.

"What is it?" he asked.

"*I've* seen your face."

"Yes, you have," he said. "But I didn't bring you here to kill you. Regardless, you're not leaving anytime soon. You are not leaving ever."

I looked ahead with a steely gaze.

"Where's the bathroom?" I asked.

"Right in here," he said, pushing open a large oak door. "Through the bedroom."

Gav

I watched as she walked into my bedroom. Her eyes darting everywhere, so curious. Her gaze picking across my bedstand, my dresser, my walls. It was strange to see the room as she saw it, with new eyes. I saw myself reflected in her sight: a clean monster. A tidy villain. A serial killer with good taste in linens.

In the bathroom, she rushed to the window and I almost yelled out. She stood there silently, though, her fingers on the sill, looking outside. The pine branches in the nearby forest waves slowly at us.

"It's a two story drop from this window," I said from behind her. "Don't try to escape."

Why did I have to be the killjoy? The realistic one, always. I'd killed off her fantasies left and right already.

"I won't," she said softly, still eyeing the forest beyond the windowsill. "I wouldn't fit through the window, anyway."

True enough. My eyes swept down over her backside. Her hips, wide and curving. I longed to run a hand across them. Not yet, though. A long dark smudge of dirt ran down the back of one leg, stopping at the ankle. On closer inspection, she was filthy. That wouldn't do. She would have to wash up first. Not now, but maybe later.

"Don't be too long," I said, closing the door. I heard the lock click shut, then the sound of running water in the sink. I sat on my bed and waited for her to be done. It didn't take long for the door to click open. She looked back once, longingly, at the trees through the window.

"It's beautiful outside," she said.

"It is," I agreed. Her eyelashes flitted up, dark brown lashes framing dark brown eyes. I called her kitten, but those were a puppy's eyes: innocent and desirous. They made me want to do terrible things, wonderful things. I grabbed her roughly by her uninjured arm, more roughly than was necessary.

"Back to the basement with you," I said, shutting the door on the emotions that threatened to seep from the watertight compartment inside of me. I did not want to kill her. I wanted more. So much more than I could ever have.

So much more than I could ever deserve.

CHAPTER NINE

Kat

The hours blended into each other. It had been two days since I had gotten kidnapped. Two? Or three? I could feel the effects of my meds beginning to ebb. Anxiety was creeping back into my body.

In the darkness of the basement my fingers twitched as I huddled against the wall. Blind as I was, I could almost conjure up the vision of the pill bottle in my mind. The feeling of twisting the hard plastic lid off, digging through the cotton balls for the tiny small pills that would calm me down.

There was no calm here, and I breathed slowly, trying to keep myself from having a panic attack. As much as most people mind the dark, I didn't particularly care whether or not I had a light on in the basement. When I was a kid, I never had to have a nightlight. I loved building fortresses under my bed and hiding there.

Kat, you can keep calm. Breathe in. Breathe out. The darkness was actually quite soothing.

The door opened with a sharp crack, light pouring in. I started back, my breaths catching in my throat. The anxiety I'd been trying so hard to suppress flooded my system, and my heart pumped harder. My limbs wanted to run, but there was nowhere to go.

His silhouette filled the doorway, and when he

stepped forward I saw that he had brought food - bread, cheese, and a package of dry salami.

"Good afternoon, Kat," he said.

"Is it afternoon?" I couldn't tell the difference between dawn and dusk, trapped as I was below the house with not even a single window to look out of. Why had I tried to escape? I could have had a window, at least, down here. Now I had nothing.

"It's getting late," he said. "Getting closer to your birthday, actually. I thought we might have a trade."

"I don't have anything to trade," I said mechanically.

"You have a lot to trade," he said. "Your obedience, for one. Do what I want you to do."

"Why?"

"It will make me happy."

I glared daggers at him. If he wasn't joking, he was an idiot.

"Do you really think I care at all about making you happy?" I asked.

He tilted his head.

"You're a strange creature, kitten," he said. "Let's try this again."

He strode forward and dropped the food on the blanket in front of me. The smell of the salami wafted through the dim room. It made my mouth water. I reached out for it and he slapped my hand away.

"Not yet, kitten," he said. "Not until I say you can eat. You must be obedient, you understand?"

I trembled, my nerves shot through from not being able to take my medication. Another game, that's all this was for him.

Well, I wasn't going to play his game. Not anymore.

"Can I eat?" I asked flatly. He wasn't going to hurt me without some trouble.

"No," he said.

I leaned back against the wall, crossing my arms. Breathe in, breathe out. You can stand up to him, Kat.

"Awful waste of steps to come all the way down here with food to *not* feed me. Were you just getting your exercise for the day?"

"Saucy girl."

"How about you go back up to the kitchen and bring down some chocolate cake so I can *not* eat that, too? Your quads will thank you."

He frowned and began to gather the food back up in his arms. My stomach growled, the ache shooting up through my body. I reached out and touched his arm, and he froze.

"I'm sorry," I said softly. "It's my meds. I don't have my meds. I get nervous."

Under my fingertips, his muscles were hard.

"Please," I said, my stomach growling again, even louder.

"Ask me to feed you," he said.

What? I blinked at him. What was he doing down here? The smell of the salami was seriously making my stomach churn, though, and I was definitely rethinking my earlier stance on his game. If all he wanted was to feed me... it was weird, sure, but it wasn't what I thought he was going to ask for in exchange for food.

"I—will you feed me?" I asked.

"Yes," he responded, and sat in front of me on the

basement floor, cross-legged. "What do you want to eat first?"

"The—the salami?"

"With cheese as well?"

"Um, yes."

I watched as his long fingers broke off a piece of cheese and then wrapped a piece of salami around it. He leaned forward and offered it to me. I opened my mouth and he slid the food inside.

Like a pet, I thought. I was an obedient little pet. That's what he wanted. The taste of cheddar and meat made me even hungrier, though, and I swallowed fast, opening my mouth again for the next bite.

Slowly, bite by bite, he fed me the whole pack of salami. At the end he produced a bottle of water and held it to my lips. I drank, water spilling from my lips and dribbling down my cheeks, my neck. He paused and wiped off the trickle of moisture with the back of his fingers.

"Good, kitten?"

I nodded.

"Excellent. You're learning. This is a good trade. You do one thing for me, I do one thing for you. Thank you for obeying so well. Is there anything you want, now?"

I looked up at him. That? That had been *me* doing *him* a favor? How weird.

"I won't let you go," he said quickly. "Don't ask for that. You know I can't do that."

"I want you to answer a question for me," I said, licking my lips. The traces of fatty meat and cheese lingered on my tongue.

"Yes?"

"What *are* you going to do with me?"

He paused, and I thought he might be angry, but when he spoke again, there was only confusion in his voice.

"I don't know," he said.

"You—you haven't thought it out?"

"I never had this problem before, kitten. For now, I'm going to keep you here." He didn't look irritated with me. More amused, if anything. I didn't understand it.

"But they'll be looking for me."

"Not here," he said, chucking me under the chin. "We're safe."

Safe. That was one way to describe it. Anger bubbled through me. He hadn't even thought of what he was going to do with me. For some reason, that indifference upset me more than if he had told me any of his terrible plans.

"So you don't know."

"Sorry, kitten," he said, standing up to go.

"Wait," I said. "That's not a fair trade."

He looked back at me.

"You didn't answer my question," I insisted. "Can I have something else?"

"What?"

He hadn't agreed, but I blustered ahead anyway. If this was a game of fair trade, I was going to get my share of the bargain.

"Something to wear," I said. "It's cold down here in my underwear."

He didn't even pause for a second at my request.

Immediately, he stripped his t-shirt off and threw it down at me. I saw his broad shoulders in silhouette, his bare chest gleaming in the dim light. Blood rushed to my cheeks and I looked down at his shirt quickly, grasping the soft fabric in my fingers.

"You won't fit into my pants," he said. "We'll find you something else to wear later. For now, will that do?"

I nodded and pulled the shirt over my head. It smelled like him—a faint scent of deodorant and musk. The shirt was tight across my chest, but I was grateful to be covered up at all.

"Good trade, kitten," he said, and left me sitting in his shirt on the basement floor.

Gav

A good pet. She was learning to be obedient. Maybe soon she would learn to obey more, to be mine fully and truly. Maybe I would convince her that staying inside was for the best.

Later that evening, I brought her up to the bedroom again for her to use the bathroom. I would have to convince her to stay of her own accord, or else I would forever be distracted by her needs. As of now, she was like a pet that needed constant looking after.

Cats, at least, were independent creatures, but I had to watch over her for every one of her physical needs. And tonight... I needed to find something for her to wear. Not just a shirt. The soft curves of her backside peeking out from under the bottom hem made me stir inside in a way that even her bare undergarments hadn't.

And she would have to wash soon.

The shadow hadn't come around yet. It normally stayed away for a few days after a kill, but I hadn't even thought about it since she had come to the house.

Caring about her was starting to distract me.

Kat

He let me up into the bathroom again, and I made sure to lock the door behind me. In the bathroom, I scrounged around and found what I had been searching for earlier. There was a spare razor blade at the back of a cabinet drawer, hiding in the pine board gap. It was old and rusted, but it would serve its purpose.

He could think that I was an obedient little pet, but I wasn't going to let his game get between me and freedom. As stupid as I'd been before, I wasn't going to be stupid now that I was in real trouble.

Chickenshit. Boring. I was not that person. Not anymore. I wasn't going to wait here for a Prince Charming to come save me from this monster. I was going to save myself. That's what Jules would do. That's what I needed to do.

If he didn't know what he was going to do with me, I'd have to figure out how to escape before he decided to use me as a torture experiment.

I used the rusty edge of the razor to slit open the

side of my bra and tucked it through the slit carefully, between the padding and the wire. I pulled his shirt back over my head and looked in the mirror. You couldn't see the outline of the razor; the padding of the bra hid it well.

If I had to use it, I would. On him or on me.

Preferably on him.

CHAPTER TEN

___Kat___

I opened my eyes, lying on the basement floor. The blanket was bunched under my neck and my arm was still handcuffed to the pipe. My ankle twinged slightly with pain, and the only rays of light that came into the room were from under the basement door.

It was my birthday.

The meds had worn off, and I didn't know how long I'd been out. Anxiety surged through me, and as I sat up my arm twisted and hurt. He'd said he was going out, and that's why he had to cuff me. My wrist screamed in pain, and as much as I tried to do my deep breathing, nothing was working to stop my nerves from shooting panic signals across my brain.

I raised my head as Gav opened the door, half relieved to see him, half terrified. He had a bowl of something in his hands, and I smelled the oatmeal as he crossed the room. I lifted my arm weakly.

"My wrist hurts," I said. "Take off the handcuffs."

"You must obey first," he said. "We'll eat breakfast now."

He spooned up a bite of oatmeal and held it out in front of my face. Panic gripped me in a vise. I didn't want this to be the rest of my life. I didn't want to be his pet.

"Please," I said. "It hurts—"

His hand whipped across my cheek so quickly that the sting of the slap came before I could realize he was lifting a hand to me. The spoon clattered in the bowl. My cheek stung hot, and a wave of panicked anger rose up, closing off my throat.

"Obey first, kitten," he said, lifting the spoon again. "Then we will trade."

I stared baldly at the spoon, hate boiling inside of me so hot that I couldn't think straight. All I knew was pain and hunger, and I didn't want to be here and I didn't want him to feed me.

"No," I said.

He grabbed my chin and lifted it, gripping my mouth so that my lips pursed.

"Eat, kitten," he said, bringing the spoon to my lips.

"No!"

Not today. I wouldn't be his pet today. I whipped my head sideways and kicked out. The bowl of oatmeal overturned, spilling everywhere.

Before I could be pleased about the results of my rebellion, his arm was under my armpit, dragging me up the side of the wall. I yelped as he shoved me back and pressed the spoon against my lips.

"Stop," I whispered. Panic was making my legs shiver and shake.

"Obey," he said, through gritted teeth.

"Stop," I cried. "Let me go!"

"You know I can't do that, kitten," he said. His thumb scooped the oatmeal out of the spoon, and then he shoved it into my mouth. His thumb ground against my teeth and oatmeal dripped out of the sides of my lips.

"Stop!" I sobbed. "Please, stop!"

He didn't, though. Throwing the spoon aside, he tilted my head up. At first I thought he was going to force feed me more, but then his lips crashed down on mine.

The kiss stole my breath, his body pressing the air out of my lungs. My body burned with pain, and I twisted under him, but he held me fast. The feelings that my meds would have cut off sprung into high alert, and at the same time so too did my body.

Traitor body, to respond to his kiss that way. The same way as it had responded the first time I had pressed my lips to him. The burn in my body was no longer just pain, but an aching lust. As he deepened the kiss, his tongue tracing the outline of my lips, I arched back against the wall, trying desperately to convince myself that I didn't want any part of this.

I didn't, of course. I couldn't help the sharp ache that began to press against me from the inside as he pressed against me from the outside. His hands held my arms back at the wrists, and I was only grateful that he didn't slide them up my bra to where the razor was hiding.

The razor. I couldn't let him know.

He broke away from the kiss, his eyes burning with an emotion I hadn't seen in him before. It lasted only a split second before the curtain fell again and his eyes turned on me flatly, expressionless. His arms hung limply at his sides.

"You wasted a trade, kitten," he said. "Wasted food, too."

I gulped. A tear had found its way to the corner of

my eye and began its slow journey down my cheek. I wiped it away. I did not want him to see me cry.

The anxiety was gone, replaced by hatred and rage. At least I could do that. I might have been able to attack him with the razor, but it was better to wait until he uncuffed me. I would have a better chance, then.

"I had hoped that we would have a better day today, kitten," he said. "Yesterday was so promising."

He waited for me to say something, but there was nothing else to say. He gathered the upturned bowl and the spoon from the floor, and went to leave without uncuffing me.

"It's your birthday," he said, and I was surprised that there was no hint of anger in his voice. "I'll be back later with your present. It would be better for you if you obeyed me then."

Gav

Of course, her birthday. She would respond better once she saw that I was going to treat her well on her birthday. I should have started with that, maybe. Now I had to find a present that would suit her.

I dug through my closet upstairs. There had been something I'd found a while back, a box of jewelry from my mother. I'd stolen it and hidden it away after she'd died. My fingers touched something hard in the back of the shelf, and I pulled out the rosewood box. It gleamed a dark red where I brushed the dust off of it.

Opening the box, I took out the necklace. A silver necklace, two hearts intertwined. I remember my mother wearing it, the silver chain sparkling around her throat. Her throat…

Her throat was cut. My father held the knife. Blood, blood everywhere.

The box clattered to the ground, spilling the other jewelry across the floor. The shadow swirled up, the darkness invading the bedroom. *No.* I did not want the shadow here. Not again. It was too soon.

The silver chain in my hands dug into my skin, but I clutched it all the tighter. I closed my eyes but I could still feel the shadow there, waiting patiently at the periphery of my eyes. Waiting for me to find it again. In my hand, the thin metal hearts seemed to beat. *Mother. Mother. My mother…*

I howled, and the sound echoed through the empty, empty house.

Kat

The razor had cut through the bottom of my bra, and I was adjusting it so that it wouldn't poke out when the light on the stairs came on. Hastily shoving it back underneath the padding, I leaned back against the wall, my arm twisted up and hanging limply from the pipe.

Gav pushed open the door slowly. Still topless. He hadn't put another shirt on. I didn't know whether or not he was trying to show off his muscled chest, or if he actually didn't care. From what I knew about him, I'd have to guess the latter.

Now, he was holding something in his hands. A present, he'd said. He came to me and held it out. It was a necklace. A silver chain, dangling from his fingers. The heart charms hanging off the end gleamed brightly in the thin light.

"Here," he said. "Your present."

"You didn't wrap it," I said. I wasn't going to play this particular game, not after he had chained me back up to the pipe.

He paused, and as his face turned halfway to the light I could see that his eyes were rimmed red under his dark lashes. Had he been crying?

"Do you want me to wrap it?" he asked. His voice was small, confused. In his fingers, the necklace turned, the hearts spinning at the end of the chain.

"I don't want it," I said. I tried to sound confident, but for some reason I couldn't make my voice raise any higher.

"Why not?"

"Because I want to leave."

"You can't leave. You can have this, though. It's a gift." He sounded pleading.

"I don't want any gifts from you. I hate you."

I pushed his hand away, and the necklace swung like a pendulum. Before I could say anything else, he'd taken my hand and twisted it down and behind my back. I could feel the chain cutting into my skin between our hands, even through the bandages that covered my cuts. In my bra, the razor turned and pushed against the fabric. I hoped that it wouldn't cut through to my skin.

He kissed me hard, and as he kissed me he pressed into me. I could feel his erection growing through the fabric of his pants, pressing against my thigh. His obvious attraction sent a shudder of uncalled desire through my body. His bare chest was hard, his muscles rippling under the pressure between our bodies.

Hot, it was so hot. I struggled to breathe and he tilted his head, letting my lips go and pinning me back so that his forehead was against mine and our faces were only inches apart.

"You're attracted to me," he said.

"I still hate you."

"Why do you hate me?" he asked. His skin was smooth against mine, and his breath was fresh, like spearmint. I hated to even think about how bad my breath smelled, but he nuzzled against me as though it was no problem at all. I struggled to get away from him but he held me fast.

"You're a monster," I said.

He paused before speaking.

"Maybe."

"Maybe? You kill people!"

"Kitten, these men are not good men that I kill. They are wifebeaters. They are child abusers. They pay off judges and slip through the cracks. They're the real monsters. Sometimes I go to their funerals and watch their family weep... with relief."

"How can you tell?" I asked. I wasn't sure if I believed him. Isn't that what any serial killer would say? Don't they always blame their victims? But maybe if he thought what he was saying was true... maybe he wouldn't kill me.

"I can tell any emotion," he said. He brought his free hand up to my cheek and caressed my jawline with his thumb. "That's how I know what you truly feel about me."

"You disgust me," I whispered.

"In part, yes. But I also attract you, even now. My touch thrills you. You want me to take you, to fuck you."

"No."

He stepped back. Amusement danced in his eyes again.

"No, not yet. Not right now. But you will. And when you want it, I'll be here waiting. Until then, take my present." He held out the necklace again, and again I heard a softening in his voice.

"Will you take off this handcuff?" I asked.

His eyes flickered over, and I believe it was the first time he realized then that I was still locked to the pipe. He stepped forward and took off the cuff without another word.

Free. I had both hands. I rubbed my sore wrist, my upper arm feeling for the spot where the razor was. Now, maybe. If I had the chance—

"Take it," he said, holding out the chain.

I reached out and took the necklace, my fingertips brushing against his. Despite myself, I felt a thrill when he touched me. Damn him! Damn myself! I coughed and turned my attention to the charm, hoping that he wouldn't see the evidence of my attraction in my face.

"Where did you get this?" I asked.

"It was my mother's."

"Where does she live?"

"Nowhere. She's dead. I was looking through her

things."

I didn't dare ask the question that was floating through my mind: *Did you kill her?* Then I remembered the noise I'd heard from upstairs.

"Was that why I heard you screaming before?"

His eyes flashed down to mine, and there was danger in them. A frightened anger. I had stepped into something I didn't understand, and there was more here than I wanted to know.

"I wasn't screaming." His voice was hoarse, too quiet. It sounded like the rasp of a rattler's tail before it lashed out to strike.

"Fine," I said quickly.

"Do you want to wear it?" he asked.

I nodded. I didn't want to make him angrier than he already was. I could sense that he was on the edge of lashing out, and I sure as hell didn't want him to lash out at me.

He took the necklace back, and again I felt the brief thrill of his touch on my hand. He unclasped the chain and motioned for me to turn around.

Facing the back wall, my hand moved up under the shirt I was wearing. My fingers touched the outline of the razor. I could pull it out now. I could whip around, slice through the air, slice through his throat. If I aimed right, I could cut his jugular and escape, run, run—

His fingers slid under my hair, brushing it to one side. At his touch, I shivered. The sight of his teary eyes, the tremble of his voice—I couldn't do it. Not now. Something held me back.

Maybe it was that I wasn't a killer myself. Maybe I was scared that it was dark, and if I messed up I would ruin my one chance at escape. Maybe I felt sorry for him. Whatever the reason, my fingers retreated, leaving the razor tucked safely in the bottom of my bra.

He brought the chain over my head, encircling my neck. On the nape of my neck I felt his knuckles graze my skin as he closed the clasp shut. If I closed my eyes, I could imagine that we were a married couple, and he was helping me get ready for a dinner party. A sense of security swept through me, a warm feeling. The strangest feeling.

Gavriel bent his head and kissed my naked shoulder, his lips trembling almost imperceptibly against my skin. Kissed me like a husband, like a gentle lover. His words were a whisper that floated faintly to my ear in the darkness.

"Happy birthday, kitten."

CHAPTER ELEVEN

Gav

Why was I so interested in her? It made no sense. There was a spark of something inside of her that drew me from behind the dark shadow to peer out. No other woman had ever been able to draw me out.

It wasn't only that I didn't love the women I brought home. It was more than that. I hated them. Every one of them. Gold-diggers. Idiots. They looked at me and saw that they wanted to see, and didn't look any further. With a suit on, I was their fantasy - a smoky billionaire tempting them into bed, a lawyer whispering dreams of Paris into their ears, a young CEO who would sweep them away from their boring, useless lives.

That, perhaps, was why she drew me out. She had looked at her boring, useless life and tried to escape it without anyone to help her. She'd taken a look at the world and said... no.

I admired that.

Some might say that suicide is for cowards. I dare them to hold a razor to their wrists and say it as they slice into their own flesh.

There aren't a lot of things out there that scare me. I've put a knife through a man's heart. I've seen blood spurt and froth forward from the lips of the dying on my table. And yet the thought of killing myself terrifies me, sends a shudder out from my hands and through my arms.

The shadow smiles inside me. It knows that there is only one other thing that terrifies me, and that's running out of people to kill.

I clasped the necklace around her, caressing her collarbone, and thought that she was doing very well. The handcuff was gone from her wrist, but this silver chain was one that would bind her even more tightly to me. There were still some secrets she had yet to reveal to me, but I knew I would be able to take her soon. Then she would be mine, mine for good.

Mine forever.

"Come upstairs, kitten," I said to her, turning her gently around. "I have another present for you."

Kat

Following Gavriel up the stairs, I wondered if he knew about the razor. It wouldn't have surprised me to know that he was simply teasing me. How could I use it, anyway? If I held it wrong, or not tightly enough, all I would do is injure him. And anger him.

I didn't want him to be angry at me. I saw what he did to people who angered him. Whether it was true or not that he only killed bad people, I thought he could probably find an excuse to kill the girl who'd witnessed him murdering someone.

He led me up through the house. Every step I took

was slow, savored. The light was bright here, and though it burned my eyes I couldn't get enough. I'd been stuck down in the darkness for too long. Maybe if I let him do what he wanted to me, he would let me out from there. Maybe—

No. I wouldn't sell myself for a better cage. I steeled myself and continued up the stairs behind him. He let me into the bathroom, and I took my time. I put toothpaste on my finger and used that to brush my teeth. I wasn't about to use a serial killer's toothbrush, no matter how bad my breath smelled.

When I went to leave, though, he stopped me and walked past me into the room.

He sat at the edge of the bathtub and turned on the faucets. Steaming water poured into the cream colored granite tub. I stood in the doorway and watched.

"What are you doing?" I asked finally. Gav looked up as though surprised I was still there.

"You're going to take a bath," he said. "That's your second present, kitten."

I almost melted inside. It had been nearly a week since I'd bathed.

"Thank you," I said. He stayed, though, and when the bath was full he made no movement to leave.

"Are you going to stay and watch?" I asked, frowning.

"I'm going to help," he said.

All the breath ran out of my body, and I crossed my arms.

"I can take a bath myself."

"Are you going to clean yourself with those bandages on both hands?"

I looked down to where the bandages were dirty and beginning to pull off.

"Maybe."

"You can't get water on those stitches. They'll get infected." He spoke matter-of-factly, as though it was a simple problem with only one solution.

"I don't—"

"What, kitten?"

"I don't want you to see me naked," I said, hating the timidity in my voice.

"That's too bad, isn't it?"

"But—"

"No, kitten." He stood up from next to the bathtub. "Do you need me to help you undress?"

"No!" I nearly screamed the word. I couldn't risk him finding the razor in my bra. "No, I'll—I'll get undressed."

Turning away from him, I stripped quickly, balling up my bra so that the razor was well-hidden. My mouth was dry as I turned around, completely naked. I could feel the heat coming from my cheeks where I blushed hard. I hated being naked in full-light.

Stupid, maybe, to be self-conscious standing in front of a serial killer. But I couldn't help it. His eyes swept over my body, over every roll of fat, every lumpy part that wasn't supposed to be lumpy, over my unshaved legs and my unshaved...well, you know. I waited for him to tell me how disgusting I was, to order me into the bathtub.

Instead, he licked his lips.

"You are... incredible," he said.

My jaw dropped. I tried to hide my surprise as he

reached out and helped me step into the bath. As soon as my feet touched the water, all of my other thoughts disappeared. I slid down, letting my body sink down into the deliciously hot water. Steam rose in white billowing clouds around us, fogging the bathroom mirror.

I closed my eyes. My feet rubbed against each other underwater. It felt so good. I could almost forget where I was, who was with me. When I opened my eyes, though, he was watching me intently. He coughed slightly.

"Thank you for being obedient," he said. "Now another trade."

Another trade. My heart beat faster. What was he doing to me? I had never responded like this to a guy before, any guy. But the low rumble of his voice sent my heart into palpitations like I was some horny teenager. The confidence in his voice, the way he moved, the way he spoke with such sureness. There was nothing I could do but clamp down on it as hard as I could, to try and push the feeling back.

"You let me wash you, and in return I'll put on new bandages for all your cuts. Yes?"

"Yes," I whispered.

He took a washcloth and dipped it in the hot water. The bar of soap he picked up was one of those luxurious handmade soaps, cut like vanilla fudge. It smelled just as good, too. When he touched the washcloth to my back, my lips dropped apart. I couldn't hold back a long sigh as the cloth moved over my shoulders, rubbing my skin in long slow circles.

"Good, kitten?" he whispered. I shook my head yes. Obedient, that's what he wanted. That's what I would be, until I had my chance.

He washed my back, then my neck, being careful around the silver chain. For some reason, he hadn't asked me to take it off before bathing. I supposed that it was real silver.

The bandages peeled away without hurting, and his hands moved carefully around the cuts on my arms. The hot water only made me wince a few times, when the washcloth came too close to the fresh cuts made by the glass window. I wondered if the cuts made him think about how I had tried to escape.

He unwrapped the bandage off of one of my hands and washed around it. His fingers massaged my fingers one by one, the cloth cleaning between the cracks. The feeling was so sensual that my pulse began to quicken. He massaged the thick heel of my palm just under the deep cut, the cloth clouding the water with soap. Then he stopped, his hand still holding my wrist.

"Your wrists are the only places on your arms that you didn't cut," he said. He held them up higher in the light, and I knew then what he was seeing. Fear turned my blood cold. I tried to pull away, but not in time.

"They were cut before, though," he said. "There are scars here. Along both wrists."

He took my hand and ran his thumb over the white seam. I watched him carefully, looking for signs of anger. Instead, when he turned his face up, there were tears in his eyes. He blinked them back, but not before I could see them.

"What is this, kitten?" he asked. His voice broke my heart, it was so tender. I had to remind myself that this was the same man who had used a saw to cut a body into pieces on his kitchen table.

But this man was different from the one I had seen through the window. He seemed... gentle. Despite myself, I felt my heart opening up.

"I— I tried to commit suicide once," I said.

"When?"

"When I was fifteen."

He paused, and I tried to read the emotion on his face. His eyes shone a deep blue-gray in the fog of the hot water. I couldn't tell what he was thinking. Was he pitying me? Was he annoyed with me? I wanted desperately to know, but as soon as I saw a bit of him open up, he pulled back and wore a mask of indifference.

"Was that why you ran away? Because you tried to commit suicide and failed?"

I turned my head up sharply.

"How do you know about me running away?"

"How do you know about that?" he repeated, mocking me lightly. "Come on, you work in a library. I looked it up."

I pulled my wrist away from him and he let my hand go. The scars throbbed as I remembered the day I had tried to commit suicide. The note. The knife.

"Thanks for reminding me I failed," I said.

"Failed miserably. You're much more alive than most people."

Raising my eyes to his, I was met with a blank stare. I didn't know what he meant by that. I didn't feel alive. I was a prisoner. It didn't sound like an insult, though, and I flexed my hand, trying to get rid of the phantom ache.

"Did you know about my suicide?" I asked.

"Before, I mean?"

"They don't keep juvenile records on public file. I only noticed the scars."

He shuddered, and I felt emboldened.

"I cut myself," I said. I don't know why, but I wanted him to know all of the details. He didn't seem to want to know, but I didn't care. "In a bathtub, so it would be easy to clean up."

"You see, this is why I couldn't leave you alone in the bathroom," he said, the joke falling flat. Then he turned serious again, his eyelashes fluttering down on his cheeks. He moved to my side, the bar of soap gliding over my shoulder. My breath went shallow as he touched my neck.

"Did it hurt, kitten?"

The scar throbbed again, and I clamped back on the feeling. Was he being nice to me in order to manipulate me? I wanted to reach out to him, but I didn't want him to have control over me. Not like that. I pressed my lips together before speaking.

"It hurt less than I thought, and I felt myself just— slipping away"

"Yes."

"That's why I'm not so scared. To die, that is. It was… peaceful."

A smile tugged on the corners of his mouth.

"What?"

He looked up at me, his hand falling back from my skin.

"The way I kill people, it's not peaceful for them."

I jerked away from him, the water splashing at the edge of the tub.

"Why would you say that?"

"Say what?"

"Why would you say that to me? That you wouldn't kill me peacefully? Or—"

"Oh, I wouldn't kill you at all," he said, raising his eyebrows as though he was surprised my conclusion.

"But you kill others. Torture them."

He smiled sadly and wrung hot water over my shoulder. The washcloth felt rough against my skin, and I wanted his hand back on me, as much as I hated to want it.

"I told you, kitten, these are not good men that I find. I need to kill, and if anyone has to die, it is a good thing that it is them."

I looked back down at my wrists. The white scar almost glowed against the redness of my skin in the heat of the steam.

"Have you ever thought about it?" I asked quietly. "Suicide?"

"Killing myself?" He laughed out loud, and the sound echoed against the bathroom tiles. It was such a strange reaction, but his laugh made me want to laugh along, that's how infectious it was. "God, no. That's abnormal."

"Abnormal?"

"I'm not judging," he said, spreading his hands. "It's simply abnormal."

I blinked hard. His reaction took me completely aback.

"I can't believe a serial killer thinks I'm abnormal."

"Take it as a compliment. Most people are like me: we enjoy life. Or at the very least, we don't want it taken away from us. I think that's what joy is."

"I can't... I don't..."

"Don't worry, kitten," he said, smiling. "But answer another question for me, please. A trade, if you like."

"Sure," I said, shaking my head in disbelief. It felt crazy to have a serial killer laughing at me for trying to kill myself. Then again, there wasn't anything that wasn't crazy about this whole situation.

"Tell me, kitten," he said, still smiling boldly at me, "why exactly did you try to kill yourself?"

Gav

Delicious, her body. The water turned the pale skin pink, reddened her cheeks in the white fog of the water. She held her arms up obediently on either side of the tub, the bandages only a few inches above the waterline. I kept waiting for her hands to slide down accidentally toward the water, but they never did.

She was perfectly in control of her body. I could see it from the way she moved. Carefully, her toes tested the water, slipped in only when she was sure that it wouldn't burn.

I wouldn't burn you, I wanted to say. *I wouldn't hurt you.*

Of course, that wasn't quite true.

"Why did you try to kill yourself?"

It was a simple question, but from the way she reacted I could tell that it was one she hadn't had to answer in a long time. Her plump pink lips parted, her chestnut hair darkening almost to black at the roots from where her sweat had moistened it. A strand of hair lay stuck to her neck, and I wanted to brush it away and kiss the spot it had left.

"I was bored," she said.

"Of life?"

"Yes." The word slipped out past her lips, and she stared as though watching it go. I was silent. I wanted to listen. I wanted to understand.

"I hated my parents," she said. "My stepdad was horrible, and my mom didn't stop him when he…"

She waved her hand at me as though I knew what was in that lacuna - a lifetime of abuse, maybe, or some kind of emotional torment. The memories choked in her mouth, and she looked down. Was she looking at her body under the clear hot water? Or was she trying to find her reflection there between the ripples?

The silence was broken by a single drop of water falling from the faucet into the tub. Her head jerked up and she continued as though reawakened.

"I didn't like anything… anything at all. It was like the world was empty, black and white instead of color, like you said. Mostly black."

"Black?"

I thought of my shadow creeping in on the edges of my life, narrowing my focus until I could think of nothing else but how to get rid of it.

"Nothing looked like it used to. Food didn't taste like food. I'd eat an apple, and halfway through I would realize that I had been eating it. I would go out with my friends, and they'd all be laughing and happy. I'd laugh, too, because I didn't want them to know that there was this thing that was wrong with me. But there wasn't anything inside. I imagined my heart inside my chest, and there was nothing but a hole there."

She looked up at me, the shine that meant sadness in her eyes. Lifting my hand, I wiped her cheek as solemnly as a priest. Saying nothing. This was her confession. She swallowed, all the while searching my face as if I had the answer.

"And I was curious."

"Curious?" I raised one eyebrow, encouraging her on.

"To see if there was anything else. Anything more that happens after... this world is over."

I lowered the washcloth.

"And?"

"And?"

"Is there anything else?"

I realized that I had been holding my breath as I asked the question. As though this girl, this beautiful young woman in my cage, could give me the answer to something I had long decided had no answer. Strands of hair fluttered loose as she shook her head.

"I didn't actually kill myself. My parents found me before I could die."

"But did you see anything at all?" I leaned forward. Her eyes were deep pools; I could trust her. Had she found truth, somewhere beyond this world? It was what I hoped, what I feared. "Did you get close?"

Biting her lip, she blinked away the last of her tears. My pulse was pounding, and I thought that she could hear my anticipation, so loud was the beating of my heart. The seconds drew out; I clenched the cloth in my hand.

"No," she said finally, looking surprised at the emotion in my face. "No. There's nothing after this."

I turned away from her to breathe out my disappointment. The stone of the granite tub felt warm under my hand, like a living thing.

"Gavriel?" she asked.

My face snapped shut as I smiled at her. No more. I would draw her out as much as I could, but I could not risk drawing myself out.

"You remind me of a poem," I said. "The last lines of a poem. Would you like to hear them?"

She nodded. She was confused. So was I.

"*The shooting stars in your black hair, in bright formation, are flocking where, so straight, so soon? — Come, let me wash it in this big tin basin, battered and shiny like the moon.*"

Picking up the bottle of shampoo, I squeezed out a dollop into my hand.

"Come," I said. "Let me wash your hair."

Her legs tucked to her chest, she faced away from me. I cupped handfuls of water over her hair. My hands stroked her head, massaging her scalp down to the tops of her trapezius muscle. The shampoo rose in clumps of thick white foam on her dark hair. Her shoulders settled against the cream granite as I worked the shampoo through her hair, her skin smoother than any polished stone.

When I rinsed the lather from her hair, she tilted her head back into my cupped palm, the way I had held her when she was on the kitchen table. She was beginning to trust me. The curve running from her neck to her shoulder was exquisite. I longed to run my fingers over her whole body. Soon, very soon.

After so much talk of darkness, I did not realize until after I had finished rinsing her hair that the shadow had retreated from the edges of my vision.

CHAPTER TWELVE

Kat

The water stopped steaming. Gav's hands were in my hair, his long fingers teasing out the knots slowly, carefully. He slicked my hair back with more hot water, and all of the thoughts that had been drifting through my mind slowly washed away with the remnants of the shampoo.

My suicide. It felt like forever ago. How long had it been? Seven years?

I'd lied to Gavriel. My stepdad had been horrible to me, sure. He'd beat my mother and me too, sometimes. But the numbness had started creeping through my body long before then.

The first emotion to go was happiness. It went hiding one day, and I thought it would come back, but it didn't. I searched for it for a while, then one day I stopped searching. I had forgotten what it felt like, or why I was searching for it in the first place.

Then I couldn't feel sadness. No sadness, no frustration. When bad things happened, I would have to force myself to frown, as though I cared whether or not our baseball team had lost, or whether or not a character in a movie died. I didn't care when my tests started coming back with failing grades.

Anger was the last one, and I clung to it for a while, yelling at my mom for my stepdad's faults. Then even the anger left, and I was alone with nothing but a barrier in my brain that kept me from feeling a thing.

Some people can't feel pain on their skin, I read once. They touch a hot stove and don't even notice. It was like that, but with everything. It's not that the feelings were *gone,* really. They weren't. They were just buried so deep inside of me that I didn't even want to think about what would happen if they came back.

Sorrow and happiness both, sunken into the tissue of my body. Hiding under layer after layer of skin, invisible. Like an empty box wrapped and put under the Christmas tree to tease.

Unwrap me and there's nothing left.

Gavriel's hand was moving down my neck, now, the washcloth cleaning off every inch of my skin. Here, trapped in this house, trapped in this bathtub, I had nothing else to think about but the sensation of his hands on my body. I wasn't worrying about getting enough hours for work, or being able to pay off my bills. The only thing that my mind had to think about was *him*.

And oh, God forgive me, he felt *good*.

Was he evil? Truly evil? Was he good, as he claimed, killing only evil men? I didn't know, and my body didn't care.

His hands moved down and over my breasts, and I let out a small gasp as the washcloth grazed my nipple. Gav leaned forward. I could hear his breathing in my ear, and his dark hair was partially reflected in the ripples of water. But he didn't say anything.

No, he said nothing, but his hands said it all. As he switched the washcloth from one hand to another, his fingers cupped my breast, sliding back and forth, letting the weight sway in the water. Then his thumb moved up, tracing a circle over my already erect nipple.

He knew how I felt. He had to know. My breathing was shallow, and he'd done this before - back on the table. Now, though, he was more gentle, his strokes like a soft breeze over my skin. He cupped another hand of water and held it to my collarbone where the silver hearts lay against my skin, letting the hot water drip down slowly.

Before, I had struggled against him. Struggled against the straps that held me down. Now there was nothing holding me down, and yet I did not struggle.

What could I have done? You might ask this. You might forgive me for giving in. There was nothing I could have done, not really. But the truth was that I had spent the last of my willpower in our conversation, and I did not want to fight any more.

No, it was that I did not want to fight *this*. Not when the washcloth stroked my nipple so slowly, not when he squeezed my breast slightly and made me moan in the back of my throat. The ache that I had not yet gotten rid of surged between my legs, swelled in the hot water.

At the sound of my moan he nuzzled the side of my head, his mouth against the bottom of my ear. His arm crossed over my chest and held me tight as he kissed me on the neck just below my ear, and made me moan again.

I was melting in this bathtub, melting under the pressure of his hands and the heat of his breath on my skin. He kissed me again and his tongue curved out, caressing the bottom of my earlobe, sliding hot and wet until finally he sealed his lips around the lobe and sucked, his tongue still teasing the strip of flesh between his lips.

"*Ohhhh.*"

In my mind I was already making excuses, constructing a story that I would tell the world once I escaped.

I did it to make him trust me, I would say. I wanted to trick him into thinking I was attracted to him. It would be a good story, and maybe I would be able to make myself believe it, later.

If I had to stand before God, though, I would not be able to lie - I wanted him badly, wanted his tongue on more places than just my ear. Wanted him inside of me, this murderer, this kidnapper, this monster. I wanted everything he had to offer me and more.

This, too, I would lie about: when his hand slid down between my thighs, I parted my legs to give him access, I arched my back and groaned again as his fingers found me and slid down, curved, pressing perfectly against the spot where I needed relief.

Tension licked through my nerves as his mouth moved down to my collarbone, licking, sucking, breathing alternately hot and cold on my neck. His two fingers slid into my body and I whimpered as he let his teeth graze my shoulder, his lips soft and delicious and sinful, oh so sinful.

He moaned along with me as his fingers thrust deeper, then out again. His breath matched my own. It had been my choice to kiss this man and I had chosen wrong, and the penalty was the ache that he sent running through my limbs as his fingertips pressed down into me, the ache that rose and rose, never bursting, no, every time I was close he retreated and I twisted in his arms, unable to find release.

He kissed the side of my jaw as his fingers worked into me, the pressure inside of me mounting and mounting, like heat would expand out the air in a balloon. I was stretched thin, my nerves vibrating with pure desire. God, I would never admit this later, but the desire that tore at me cared nothing about the man making me desire him, cared nothing about his innocence or guilt. It wanted only release. So much pressure. So much.

My hips bucked against his hand, water splashing at the sides of the tub. Suddenly, he was gone. I gasped as he pulled his hand back, his fingers one second there and the next second not, and my body felt so empty, so open. I clutched for his arm but he was already drying off.

"What… why…" I stammered. He gazed at me levelly, and my protests died in my throat. Who was I to ask him for satisfaction? Guilt flooded my body, and my cheeks turned hot, hotter than the water in the tub that was already cooling off. We had been in the bathroom for a long time, and the suds from the shampoo had already been absorbed back into the bathwater.

"Why did you do it?" he asked.

"What?"

"Why did you try to kill yourself?"

I bit back a thousand replies. He had already gotten an answer from me, but apparently that wasn't the one he wanted.

"Why do you care?"

"I'm so used to people begging me to let them live. It's interesting to see that you swing the other way. You *want* to die."

"I *don't*," I said. Tears welled in my eyes - more from the ache still racking my body than from any kind of emotion. I needed release, and I wasn't going to get it, and damned if I was going to beg him. "Not anymore."

"What changed, kitten?" His voice was soft, sympathetic, and if I didn't know what he was I would have loved him then, even as I hated him for bringing me to the edge and leaving me there.

"Death wasn't going to make things any better for me," I said bitterly. "I decided to stay alive. I was going to leave my family. I was going to go to college. Get a good job. Get a good life. Of course, that was before a serial killer locked me in his basement and tortured me."

"Hardly torture. You flatter me."

I stared at him, mouth agape.

"You tied me up—"

"And what? Brought you close to the best orgasm you'll ever have? Such torture. I didn't let you finish? Come, now, kitten. Don't tempt me to show you what real torture is."

I clamped my mouth shut. I had no doubt that he knew how to torture. He had tortured that professor for days before killing him. My mind saw again the body on the table, the slashes, and bile rose in my throat. *How could I have let this monster touch me like that?*

"You wouldn't try to kill yourself again, would you?"

"Maybe," I shot back. "How long are you going to keep me prisoner here?"

"You're not a prisoner, you're a trespasser on my property. You've fallen into a hole in the forest. You probably won't ever get out. It's not bad. It's just life."

"Life in a cage is not a life."

"You're mixing your metaphors, kitten."

"I'm not your kitten," I spat. "You can dress me up and feed me and give me baths like I'm your pet, but I'll never be your pet."

He held out a towel to me, and I grabbed it and wrapped it around my body quickly. The ache between my thighs made my legs shake as I stood. He chuckled.

"It's a good thing your wrists aren't hurt, kitten."

"Why?"

"We're not going back to the basement."

Gav

She dried herself off quickly, then knotted the towel under her armpit. Her body was wonderful, the curve of it under the terry cloth. I licked my lips as I thought about how she would taste.

"Are you going to kill me?" she asked. Her voice was trembling, but there was still a hint of desire in there, as much as she tried to hide it.

"You keep asking me that. Does it really matter?"

"Of course it matters," she said.

"This entire time in the bathtub, you were talking about how life doesn't matter. How boring it is."

She bit her lip. Oh, my. I would have to kiss her right there. I wanted to bite her lip, too.

"I don't want to die."

"I don't want to kill you, kitten," I said, smiling

kindly, or so I hoped. "Behave, and I won't have to."

CHAPTER THIRTEEN

Kat

Would he do it? Was he going to kill me? Dizziness overtook me as I stood up from the bath, the heat turning my head fuzzy.

His hand clamped over my wrist, and I followed limply as he led me back into the bedroom. My eyes lingered on my bra lying on the bathroom floor. If only I'd used the razor when I'd had the chance. I wouldn't make that mistake again, I decided. I only hoped I had the chance.

Leaving me next to the bed, he opened his closet and pulled out an armful of clothes. There must have been a half dozen different dresses, and an equal amount of silk lingerie.

"Here," he said. "Try something on."

"Did you get these for me?" My fingers stroked the fabric of the top dress, a satin gown that looked more expensive than my last car. Beads glittered across the bodice. The dresses looked to be my size. Had he bought them specially for me? There was no way. But he looked up at me with a bright look in his eyes. Hopeful. It made me feel ill.

"I want you to wear something nice tonight," he said. "Something pretty, like you."

"I'm not pretty," I mumbled.

"You are very pretty," he said dispassionately, as though correcting me on a fact.

"Which one do you want me to wear?" I asked.

"I don't know what color you would like best," he said. "So I got a few."

He certainly had. The second dress was a scarlet red sheath that felt even silkier than the first. And there was a whole pile of them here.

"I... I don't know." He had me completely confused. Threatening to kill me in one breath, then offering me these presents in the next? Was he dressing me up so that he could cut me to pieces? It made no sense. But then again, neither did anything else he had done with me.

"This one," he said, pulling out a long strapless green gown. The fabric was gauzy, slipping through my fingers as he laid it in my arms along with a hanger of black silk lingerie. "And these."

"I—thank you," I stammered.

"Go try them on," he said.

I stepped back into the bathroom and closed the door behind me, locking it. I exhaled.

Now. It was my chance. I grabbed up my old underwear and bra and pulled the razor from its hiding place. I set it on the counter. I would have to try to kill him now. I couldn't have planned it better. He would be distracted.

I tugged on the lingerie. The bra was a smaller band than I normally wore, but the cup size was half a size larger. Surprisingly, it fit better than my normal bra. With shaky fingers I tucked the razor inside the lingerie. I didn't bother slitting the fabric to hide it inside. If I was going to do this, I needed easy access to my weapon.

My weapon. Jesus. I was actually going to do this.

Sliding the green dress over my shoulders, I smoothed down the fabric. My cleavage peeked out from under the fitted bodice, the curves casting soft shadows on my skin. My hair, half-dry, curled over the back of my shoulders. If it hadn't been for the white bandages covering my arms and hands, I would have looked like I was going to an executive cocktail party.

I opened the door and found Gavriel sitting on the bed in a clean shirt and pants. He looked up at me with such awe that I began to tremble. His eyes swept down over me, and I swear that he could see my soul. I worried that the razor was obvious, that the outline would show through the fabric. No, of course it couldn't.

The way he looked at me, though... it was as though he was more open than ever. And what was hidden behind the mask scared me even more: he desired me.

He came and stood in front of me. His eyes looked more green than gray, maybe from the reflection of my dress fabric. His hands touched my shoulders, his fingers sliding up and down lightly. Framing his vision of me. I wondered what he saw. A helpless girl, a willing victim. I would show him that I would not go gently.

"Beautiful. Thank you for wearing it for me."

He paused, looking into my face, then spoke in a low voice that hinted at flirting.

"What do you want from me?" he asked.

"What do *I* want?"

My voice was shaky, and I swore that he knew what I was planning. But he only looked at me calmly, the look of a predator who had his prey trapped. Playing with me, that's what he was doing.

"Yes," he said. "Thank you for dressing up nicely for me. Now what do you want in return?"

"I don't know. I mean, I want you to let me go. You won't do that?"

In my heart I prayed for him to say yes. Then I wouldn't have to hurt him. I wouldn't have to kill him. I wouldn't have to escape on my own.

"No," he said, equally calmly.

"Then I don't know. I don't know what I want."

His hands squeezed my shoulders gently, above the bandages. His voice whispered into my ear.

"I do."

One hand trailed down my hand, his fingertips feeling their way down to my hip. I held my breath as he passed over the place in my bra where I had hidden the razor. But he did not stop until his hand was resting on the curve just below my waist. My heart beat fast.

"I know what you want."

With his other hand he tilted my chin up. My lips parted willingly as I let him kiss me.

Only pretend, my mind screamed. That's all this was. It was only a game, all of it. But my body urged me on, enjoyed the kiss, wanted more, wanted it all. And the small voice inside of me murmured encouragement.

Yes, it said. *This is what you want. This is what you need.*

My tongue met his, hot and wanting. He cupped my cheek in one hand, cupped my ass in the other, pulled me toward him with his heat and his desire and every dangerous wonderful thing that I never had before.

Adrenaline pulsed through me, sending every nerve

to high alert. He clutched me tight and I felt the razor's edge cutting into my skin. His hands moved over my back, ran through my hair, and all the while he kissed me and I kissed back, palms against his chest, in that hopeless position of wanting more and wanting it all to be over.

Then he reached down. His hand crumpled the green gauzy fabric, pulled the hem up until it bunched at my waist. He sought the place between my thighs and found me wet and burning down there.

It was true, I wanted him. The attraction that shamed me made him believe me. He suspected nothing, because the moan that shuddered me was real when he touched me down there, let his fingers graze my swollen sex through the silk panties. Under my bra the razor was cutting me and still I pushed further, letting him kiss me harder, touch me harder.

"I've wanted you so badly," he murmured, his voice catching on the words. It was the first time I had heard any emotion in his voice. "It's never like this. It's never real."

It's not real now, I thought. Nothing was real, not the desire that burned in me and made me soak through my panties. Not the kisses he pressed down on my mouth, my neck. Not the thrill of his fingertips against my bare skin. *It was all pretend. All pretend.*

He lifted the dress up, and I dug my hands under the top to help lift it off over my shoulders. He couldn't see me reach down into the bra where I had the razor hidden. Quickly my fingers found the blade and pulled it out.

It was the pause that did it. The moment of hesitation when his arms were lifted over my head, helping me out of the dress. The split second where I was uncertain.

No, it was the blood where the razor had cut me. The red blade slipping in between my fingers, even though I clutched it tightly.

No, it was my own conscience. Every moral, every rule I'd followed for years, coming back to tell me not to do this, not to kill, not to murder.

No, it was none of these and all of these that made me fail. I don't know, not even now, not even looking back on it with clear eyes.

A breath of hesitation, and then I lunged forward with the razor, slicing it at his throat. His arm was already blocking my path, and he saw the red-silver glint of the blade, and he swatted my hand down. The razor sliced across his chest as he jumped back, cutting him. A shallow cut. Not enough.

He leapt backwards, his face snapping shut on the emotions I had been surprised to see. Blood trickled down his chest from the cut I'd made just above his left nipple. We faced each other, predator and prey, and I knew that it was over.

Like any animal, though, I would not give up. I lunged again, and he caught my upper arm where the bandages covered my cuts. Pain shot up to my shoulder and I let out a cry. He squeezed, and the world exploded white with agony. Still I held on and twisted to get out of his grasp. He pulled me around and held me against his chest. I kicked, I screamed, I tried to reach behind me with the razor to cut him again. All the while, I knew that I had failed.

Failed again.

"Drop it," he hissed in my ear. I whipped my head back to try and hit him in the face, but he only leaned back to avoid the blow. I sobbed, the razor biting into my own fingers from where I was holding it so tightly.

"No!" I moaned. It was over. I could feel the blood from his cut soaking into the back of my dress. Still I held on.

"Drop the razor, kitten," he said, "or I'll use it to cut your pretty little heart out."

I choked my sob back. That was it. I was done. It took every single ounce of effort to open my fingers, to let the razor fall from my hand. It made no sound as it landed on the carpet.

Gav

"You don't think you can trick me that easily, do you, kitten?"

She moaned in my arms. Beautiful, she was. Beautiful and cunning. I threw her down onto my bed with a force that surprised even me. She had threatened my life, and now she would have to pay.

The rope was nylon, thick and red. She screamed as I tied her wrists with the thick loops. She kicked as I did the same with her ankles. Stronger than she looked, but not as strong as me. I secured the knots tightly to the bedposts. I'd practiced them for a long while, and the more she struggled, the tighter the rope would pull.

Her arms and legs were spread apart, each one tied

to its own bedpost. Like the man in DaVinci's drawing, a perfect specimen of humankind. Her body arched against the bed as she twisted to try and escape, sobbing all the while.

Would it be surprising to know that her cunning made me want her even more? Such a smart girl. Such a beautiful woman. She had brains under that soft delicious body, and I smiled as I stripped off my shirt, stanched the blood coming from my chest, and put on a bandage. When I came back to the bedroom, she had stopped struggling, her limbs stretched out tightly.

"Please, no," she said. "Please. Gavriel."

"You've been very naughty, kitten," I said. It stung me that she had tried to kill me, stung me more than the time she'd tried to escape.

"Please. I'll do anything. Don't hurt me. Don't kill me. I promise I won't try anything else. I promise I won't try to escape. Please—"

"You lied to me, kitten," I said, sitting on the bed next to her. Her dress was torn at the top, exposing the black bra where she'd hidden the razor. I slid my hands over the fabric to make sure that she had no other surprises waiting for me. She bit her lip as my hands touched her body, cringing back from me.

"I won't—"

"You tried to kill me. *Tsk, tsk.*"

"Don't kill me," she sobbed. Fear brightened her eyes. It was good; the shadow was nowhere to be found. "Please. I'll tell you whatever you want to know. I'll do whatever you want me to do. I'll be good. We can do a trade. I'll—"

"No more trades," I said. I took hold of her dress

and ripped it down the middle, tearing it off of her. Under the green fabric, her body was pale and beautiful as I had seen it before.

"No more trades. No more begging. You tried to take what you wanted. Now I will take what I want."

CHAPTER FOURTEEN

__Kat__

He stared down at my body, and I could see the reflection of myself in his eyes. They had gone dark gray, but there was no anger in them, only a horrible, terrifying calm. Blood was smeared across his bare chest where I had cut him with the razor.

I was going to die.

It had taken one second, one bad decision, one moment's hesitation, and that was it. I closed my eyes and willed myself not to scream. Maybe he would end it quickly. The ropes bit into my wrists and ankles and my arm screamed with pain from where he had squeezed it.

"Kitten," he said. "Kitten, look at me."

I felt his weight shift on the bed, leaning over me. Terror seized me and I opened my eyes. He was there, hovering just above me, his eyes matched with mine.

"Are you scared to die now?" he asked.

"Please don't—" I started, but he brought his finger to my lips and stopped my begging.

"Do you want to live?"

Another game? Or was this a real chance that he was giving me? I nodded yes, slowly.

"Then I will let you live," he said. "See? I am not quite the monster you thought I was."

I let go of the breath I hadn't remembered holding

in. He reached over and opened the drawer from his bedside table.

"First, though," he said, "I told you I was going to take what I wanted. You call it torture, I think. But I rather enjoy it."

From the drawer he pulled out his knife.

I began to scream.

I screamed at the top of my lungs, twisting away from him as he brought the knife up to my chest. I thought of the professor, of the pieces of skin stripped away from his body. Everything around me went black - the beautiful room, the expensive decorations. In the dim light my eyes could not stop staring at the point of the knife.

"Stop moving, kitten," he said, his voice calm under my screams. He pressed one hand down, his fingers spread across my collarbone. His leg braced against my leg and no matter how I tried, I couldn't move.

He slid the knife under the middle of my bra, between my two breasts. My screams turned ragged as I ran out of breath, trying not to let my chest heave. The air had been sucked out of the room, and there was no oxygen left. I would black out. I would—

He twisted the knife up and cut my bra in half with a single quick movement.

The noise coming from my throat now wasn't a scream. It was a high-pitched whine, a keening while I tried not to move. The blade of the knife was cold against my skin, and he slid it down slowly, down over my belly. I imagined one more twist, my guts spilling out of my body.

Instead the knife kept moving down, down, until he

had slipped it under the fabric of my panties. It rested cold against me and then he moved again, yanking the knife up. I screamed again, once, but the blade only slit the fabric.

"Darling kitten," he whispered. He pulled off the scraps of silk lingerie, leaving me completely naked. I choked on my breath as he reached over me, but he only set the knife back down in the drawer and pushed it shut.

I needed my medication. I could feel myself starting to hyperventilate. The screams had taken all of my oxygen and around me the world was turning hazy.

Then he bent down and kissed me softly. All of a sudden, my world refocused on his eyes, his gray eyes. The haze receded. I could see every small detail of his face. The dark stubble on his strong chin. The curve of his eyebrows swooping low on his forehead. The hard lines of his cheeks.

"Kitten," he said, "I want you to be mine. And I will take what I want."

He kissed me again, as lightly as butterfly wings, and I did not respond. I could not respond. Every part of me was tensed, shot through with adrenaline.

"Before I am done, you'll want it too, kitten," he whispered. "I know you will. Maybe you already do."

I was shivering now, and his hand moved over my stomach, sending goosebumps rippling over my flesh.

"Cold, kitten?" he asked. "Let's start by warming you up."

He moved down, his pants sliding against my legs as he did so. One hand cradled my breast, and he squeezed just hard enough to make me moan.

"Oh, kitten," he said. "Do you already want me?"

"No," I whispered. "No, please—"

He leaned over and kissed my nipple. Then pinched it, twisting. I screamed and he released the hard nub. Then he licked it, circling it with his tongue. The soft touch of his tongue after his twisting fingers made me ache.

Then he pinched it again, harder, and rolled it between his fingers. Pinched again. Then sucked. The warmth shot through my skin.

He moved down and I tried to squeeze my thighs together, but the rope held my legs apart no matter how I twisted.

He kissed me softly all around, from my hips down to the soft patch of hair just above my slit. As he kissed me, I could feel myself growing hot, swelling between my legs.

Without warning, he sealed his lips around me and sucked hard enough to hurt.

"Ah!" I yelped. He stopped, as suddenly as he had started, and went back to kissing me, sucking little spots all around my swollen nub.

Back up to my nipples, and this time when he sucked on my nipple I imagined him sucking down there, and I ached, oh god, how I ached.

His hand slid down, his fingers parting, two on either side. His thumb pressed into the top of my thigh as he stroked me a millimeter away from where I needed it.

"Please…" I trailed off.

"Tortured yet, kitten? Maybe. Not quite enough for me. You were screaming before. You'll scream again."

He squeezed his fingers together on either side of my slit and licked, one long slow stroke of his tongue that sent me shuddering.

"*Ohhh*," I groaned.

"Don't pretend for me, kitten."

"I'm not... I'm not—"

"Hush."

He licked me again, and then his hand came back up to twist my nipple, hard, at the same time as he thrust two fingers into me. I gasped at the pain mixed with pleasure. My body didn't know how to react.

He continued. With every hard pinch of my nipple he would lick my swollen clit, then go back to stroking me on both sides with his fingers. Then he would twist my erect nipple and thrust his fingers in, and my body clenched around him, wanting more, needing more.

Sweat beaded on my forehead. The room was hot, so hot. I couldn't breathe. I wanted release. Oh god, I needed it soon or I'd faint.

"Please," I said. "Please."

He slapped me across the face and twisted both my nipples so hard it felt like burning. I screamed.

"That's the scream I want," he said. He bent his head down to my aching nub and sucked hard, his mouth sealed around me as he thrust his fingers once again into my body. Oh, god, it felt so good. I was there, I was almost there—

He pulled his fingers out.

I bucked my hips up, searching for release, but it did not come. I opened my mouth, and the scream that escaped me was a gasping scream, hoarse with desire.

"Tell me you want me, kitten," he whispered.

"Oh, god," I moaned. I couldn't. I couldn't.

He touched me on either side with his fingers and I

twisted, wanting him inside of me.

"Say it. Tell me you want me."

"No."

He pressed hard, and my body rocked into him, hips arching, but his fingers were gone, the pressure eased.

"Say it."

I moaned, the sound filling the room. Only pretend. This wasn't real. Say anything, confess everything. It didn't matter.

It didn't matter. Who would know? Who would ever think it was the truth? I opened my mouth and made my confession, and if it was true then I was the only one to know it.

"I want you."

He licked me hard, again, his tongue flicking once at the top and sending white hot shocks of pleasure through my body. I was almost there, god, I was so close—

"Say it agai—"

"I want you!" My voice was ragged, my tongue thick in my mouth. "I want you. I want you."

He twisted my nipples as he thrust his fingers in me, three short thrusts and then *out* and no! God, no, I needed it, I needed more, I needed all of him—

"Louder."

"I want you!" I screamed. "Please! I want you! I want you! Gavriel, I want you!"

He sat back on the bed, his hands no longer on me. My body shook with the ache of desire, unsatisfied. Lust tore through me, a hard pain that made my teeth chatter.

"No," I moaned. "Don't stop. Oh god, please, don't." I whimpered, unable to stop myself from pleading. This was the torture he wanted to see, this was the agony that he would leave me in. I hated him then, hated him and wanted him in equal measure, and I had never known that such desires could be one and the same.

Then he smiled, his lips gleaming with my juices.

"There, kitten," he said. "I'll be back soon."

CHAPTER FIFTEEN

Gav

Instead of satisfying her, I decided to let my kitten squirm. All tied up, looking delicious. Tasting delicious. When I took my knife out of the drawer she nearly cried, but I left her there without touching her again.

Release. That's what she wanted. That's what I wanted, too, but I could control myself. I could control her. Yes, everything was falling nicely into place. Even with her little stunt with the razor. I admired her for that. She was a smart one, I knew that from the beginning. There was something different about her that made my mind go into a reeling circle of...

Emotion? Maybe. Maybe it was the thrill of the kill, enhanced by her as a witness.

I ran a bath for myself; I wanted to imagine that I was her. Imagine what she must have felt like. In the other room she moaned, but I ignored the sounds. I wanted to know what was in my kitten's mind, what she was really, truly capable of. Now I knew she was capable of killing, or trying to kill, and I understood that. But she had also been capable of suicide.

I settled myself into the bath and picked up my knife from the granite edge of the tub. It looked bigger than when I'd used it to kill other people.

Could I do it? The shadow resting over my heart

was a poison, but could I bleed it out this way?

I put the point of the knife to my skin. The blade made a dimple on the thin tissue of skin just under the heel of my palm.

Could I do it? I wanted to. The world grew dark around me, and all I could see was the point of the knife, the shiny steel blade. I twisted the handle slightly. The knife pierced the skin and a drop of blood welled up at the point where it had slipped through into me. My teeth gritted tightly.

In the silver reflection of the blade I saw myself. My mouth twisted in horror. Pain crumpled my face. I looked almost... human.

The knife left my hand, flew across the bathtub. It hit the cream-colored stone and bounced back, slid down into the water at the other end of the bathtub. I pulled my knees back, as though the knife would come after my legs, wanting to finish what it had started.

My hand gripped the punctured wrist. It ached already, ached much more than a simple cut should have hurt. Under my fingertips I could feel the pulse of my heartbeat. It was fast, frightened, but it was there. I was still alive, after all.

Not like this. I couldn't end it like this. If I could snap my fingers and turn the world off, turn the shadow off, I would. More than her, more than anyone, I hated living. It was an endless fight against the shadow, one that I could not win. I did not want to live, no, there was nothing on earth that made me want to stay alive.

But unlike her, I was too scared to die.

I could lie to myself about why I stayed alive. I saved women from being abused. I saved children from being molested. A service to humanity. But I served the shadow only; the real reason I killed was to drive back the darkness. If I could make it go away by killing myself...

I unwrapped my fingers slowly from around my wrist. The drop of blood smeared red over my skin. I lifted the wrist to my lips and licked off my own blood. The coppery tang filled my nostrils and my stomach roiled.

I stood up from the tub. Water dripped down my body in slow rivulets; it felt thick as blood. At the bottom of the tub, the knife's edge rippled under the waterline, silver and shining.

I would never be as brave as her. No matter how much I wanted to.

How, then? The thought of popping pills repulsed me – the vomiting, the mess. A gun would be a sure thing, but again, messy. I don't know why I cared so much about my body. It was only a body, after all. I'd sink into the thick earth of a graveyard as easily as anybody else.

I forced myself to think about it. Worms devouring my flesh. The blood in my veins clotting and crumbling.

I didn't care overmuch about the bodies of my victims, but mine was different. I wanted my body to stay whole, at least until after I was dead and gone.

A stupid, irrational desire. But it *was* a desire, and I hadn't had many of those lately.

So what did that leave? Instant incineration might be a good way to go. Fire burns away the bodies I make, and it's certainly less messy. If I could find a rocket and sit under the jets, let the fire burn me to nothing in a split second, I would.

Drowning, maybe. Smothering, if you could smother yourself.

But not a knife. Not my own blood.

Enough, I thought. Her moans reached me from the bedroom, and I left the knife where it was. I had other work to do.

Kat

"Gavriel?"

"I like the way you say my name. Like you're scared of me."

"I *am* scared of you."

"Silly kitten."

He sat down on the side of the bed, completely naked except for the white towel around his waist. I hadn't realized how much I'd been pulling on the ropes that tied my hands and feet to the bedposts while Gav had been doing…what he had been doing to me. They ached.

Now he leaned over me again, and my body quivered even without his touch. His hair was wet, dark and dripping. His chin was dark, unshaven, and his eyebrows pulled together over his light eyes.

"I don't know how you did it, kitten." He turned away from me, and I longed for him to come back, despite everything. The ache had not gone away. His method of torture was terrible; I wanted nothing more than for him to return between my legs, no matter how I despised him. I did not despise his tongue.

"Did what?" I asked.

"Tried to kill yourself."

"I—what?"

"I can't do it at all. Can't even begin to cut myself." He bowed his head, his hands clasped between his legs. It was then that I noticed the prick of blood on his wrist just below his thumb.

"You tried to cut yourself? Now?" I had heard him run the bath, but I had never imagined what he was doing.

"You are brave, kitten," he said, as though he hadn't heard my question. He was off in that other place again, a place where I didn't belong. He didn't notice me staring at him, didn't notice the aghast expression on my face.

If he'd killed himself, I would have starved to death, tied to his bed. Did he even think about that? Think about me?

"The pain is worse than anything else," he said. "Not the actual pain, but the thought of leaving this behind, all of it. As much as it hurts to stay, it seems like it would hurt even more to leave. I would miss it. It needs me."

He turned to me, a shadow of pain masking his face. His fingers clutched his wrist.

"I would miss you, kitten. And the killing. I would miss never killing another person."

"That's… that's disgusting."

"No, not at all." He raised his chin up to the dimmed lights, his face beatific. "It's exquisite. The moment of release. Think about what I did to you, before my bath."

It wasn't hard to think about. How he'd touched me, kissed me. I blushed hard.

"Think about how much you wanted it, kitten."

His finger touched my bare knee, traced a line up the outside of my thigh, rested two fingers on my hipbone. My body clenched inside and I twitched my head violently back, shivers of desire taking hold of me instantly.

"I didn't—"

"Don't lie!" His voice was a roar in the quiet room. Then he became soft again. "You wanted it so badly, kitten. Think of that desire, that *want*. Think of it multiplied tenfold. How torturous it would be to deny yourself. Especially when the answer to your problem is as easy as…"

With this he leaned forward and kissed me. I ripped my lips away from his, but not before the warm wet touch of his mouth drew the desire back to me in full force. He smiled.

"Pretend you want me to stay away from you, kitten, and I will continue giving you what you *pretend* you want."

What did I want? I couldn't tell. My body had turned traitor, sided with him. Hot, wet, ready, it ached for his touch again.

"You'll sleep here from now on. With me."

My eyes met his and quickly looked away. I thought that he could see right through me, into the depths of my being, where I was beginning to convince myself that I needed him more than I needed to stay away from him.

"Aren't you afraid I'll try to kill you again?" I asked. I didn't care. But the temptation of sleeping next to his hard and muscled body... it would kill me before he did.

"Good point. We'll have to leave these ties on."

"I can't fall asleep next to a serial killer." It was useless. He had decided. Still I protested, aware even as I spoke of the futility of my demands.

"I know a remedy to help you fall asleep."

"Sticking me with a sedative again?"

He looked up at me with pure desire, fierce and hungry. His eyes were a panther's eyes, watching a helpless rabbit caught out in the open. If he had licked his chops, I would not have been surprised.

"No. Not the syringe. Something a bit more...natural."

His hand moved up from the bed and slid over my thigh, touching me where I was already slick with lust. Flames shot from my core through my limbs.

"No!" I shouted, and he removed his hand so quickly that I was left with only the memory of the pressure. I bit back a sob. God, how I wanted him!

"Have it your way, kitten," he said. He smiled at me. He knew he'd caught me already, that in my mind I was playing out the scene as I wanted so desperately for it to happen. The towel falling to the ground, his naked body hard against mine, his cock erect and pulsing between my thighs, filling the part of me that was empty, God, oh-so-empty and willing, if only my mind would play along.

He turned off the light, and we were thrown into a

dark broken only by the moonlight coming through the window. My eyes adjusted to the dim blue light as I watched him pull on a white shirt, dark briefs. His muscled backside gleamed, curving, and then was covered with fabric. He turned abruptly and I looked away, not fast enough.

Kindly, he didn't mention my watching him. Kind? Was he kind? Maybe.

One by one, he loosened the ropes at the bedposts, giving me just enough slack to be able to move my limbs, not enough to bring my hands down to my mouth, or anything else that would let me undo the knots.

"Don't move too much," he said quietly. "The ropes tighten when you pull on them."

The blanket he'd knocked to the side of the bed was light, and he tucked in the top of the blanket under my chin. He was only a shadow above me, blocking out the moonlight from the window, when he caressed my cheek with one hand. Then he kissed my forehead and slipped under the cover next to me, lying on his back, just out of reach.

CHAPTER SIXTEEN

__Gav__

My kitten lay beside me in the darkness, trying not to move. And in the darkness my heart beat underneath the bandage, pumping blood to the place where she'd cut me. In the darkness, too, my shadow waited. It was there even when I could not see it, darker still when I turned off the light. I could not hide from myself in the nighttime.

Peter Pan cried when his shadow left him. It was up to Wendy to sew it back on, to make sure that his shadow would never leave him again.

If I could leave my shadow somewhere and never see it again, I would.

My shadow. It's a darkness that creeps in, shutting out anything bright or good until all I can see is the one thing that will satisfy it and drive it away. It begins to take me over, and then all I see is evil. When I kill, it retreats.

I'm not crazy. I'm not schizophrenic. This isn't a second self or something ridiculous like that. I'm not abdicating responsibility. My crimes are my own, and I wield the knife. My stomach growls for food, but I'm the one eating. My heart aches for relief, but I'm the one murdering.

No, the shadow is something I wear like a cloak,

and like a cloak it grows heavier with each step until it's unbearable. That's when I kill. I kill. Me. Not the shadow. Still, if it were gone, I wouldn't need the release that killing gives me.

Wendy was able to sew Peter's shadow back on using only a needle and thread. Is it so impossible to think that she could cut it away from me with a razor?

Kat

When I woke up, it was dim in the room. The sky outside of the bedroom window was gray, the curtains glowing white at the edges. I longed to look outside, to see the trees now in the half-darkness. Half-turned on my side, I tugged slightly at the rope before realizing that I was still captive. The knot was still tight around my wrist.

Next to me, Gavriel kicked out. He'd fallen asleep on his back, leaving me to stare at the ceiling for hours before I finally was able to drift off into restless sleep. Now he was the restless one. He kicked again and moaned, the blanket yanked down around his waist, his body twisted.

Sweat soaked the front of his shirt, a half-circle of transparent wet fabric clinging to his sculpted chest. His brows were clenched together tightly on his forehead, an expression so painful it hurt me to watch him writhe. Both sides of his mouth turned down in a grimace. The corners of his eyes leaked tears that mixed with the sweat trickling down his temples.

Killer. Kidnapper. Torturer. But as he tossed beside me, moaning again in his sleep, he looked like a child scared of the dark.

He turned over again, a whimper escaping his lips. He murmured half-words I could not understand. Then one I could, a whisper so sorrowful it nearly broke my heart.

"Kitten," he whispered, and moaned again.

My arm was tied tight, but I could reach with my fingers as he moved his head. I touched the top of his hair, my fingertips stretching to caress him.

He stopped moaning. Stuck in an awkward stretch, I continued to pet him on top of his head with only my fingertips. My nails ran through his hair, pushing back the black mess. His lips moved but now there were no words, just silent intonations.

Then he rolled over, his arm swinging across my body, and he clutched me tightly, as though I were a pillow or a stuffed animal from his childhood. His head rested on my shoulder, damp with sweat. His knee rested on my thigh. The weight of him was so real, so impossibly human.

Was he a monster? And was I a monster for caring for him? Even now, tied up to bedposts, I could not help but think that I was less of a prisoner than he was.

I tilted my head down and kissed him softly on the forehead. Hot skin, still moist with sweat.

"Sleep," I whispered, and he obeyed.

CHAPTER SEVENTEEN

Gav

The next morning I brought her breakfast in bed. Her eyes were bleary; she must not have slept well. Pity.

"Why don't you untie me?" she asked, as I offered her a piece of buttered biscuit.

"I have to go," I said. "I can't leave you untied when I leave the house."

"Where are you going?" She wasn't eating; I was slightly irritated.

"Out."

The shadow was back. It had come back in the night, after so many days of being chased away. I knew I had to find a new victim. Not to kill right away, but soon.

There had been a man I'd been researching. A politician, one who enjoyed whoring around and beating on his wife. He'd slept with his intern, too, a fourteen year old girl. She'd come out of the building once while I was there, her hair mussed, her eyes rimmed red with tears. I watched him as he spoke with her in the parking lot, threatening her, bending her against the hood of his Lexus. The thought made me shiver with dread.

Yes. That would do it. That would drive the shadow back. An indulgence, to kill twice in a month, but I deserved it for dealing with such a hassle. That's all she was, my pet, a small hassle. I pushed the biscuit into her mouth and she chewed. Chewed, chewed and swallowed.

"What were you dreaming about last night?" she asked.

Her shoulders were relaxed, even tied up. Her lips were pink and tempting.

"I didn't dream," I said.

"You did. You were talking in your sleep."

"I don't remember."

"Were they nightmares?"

My eyes snapped back to hers. Clever one, she thought she was. And she was clever, but not clever enough. I didn't know what she'd heard last night. The screams of the man I'd been killing in my dream? The cries of my mother?

"No," I said.

"What happened to your mother?"

It was a guess, nothing more. I could tell. She was pushing, trying to figure me out. There was nothing to figure out, little kitten. Push too far, and you'll see the darkness. I tossed the last piece of biscuit back onto the plate.

"Goodbye," I said, and stood up before I could get any angrier.

The shadow was already creeping up around, clawing its way back in.

Kat

Hours passed. I struggled to untie the knots at my wrists, but I only drew the rope tighter. Hunger made my stomach growl. I wished I'd eaten more for breakfast.

What if he was serious? What if he left to try to kill himself? What if I was stuck here by myself?

Fear ran through me, and I had no way to tamp it down. Normally I would pop a pill when I got too anxious, but there were no pill here. I couldn't reach anything. The ropes tightened around my wrists and I began to breathe hard.

Calm down, Kat. Calm down. Don't freak out. If you freak out—

The door downstairs opened, and I heard his footsteps coming up the stairs. He was whistling. Strangely enough, I was relieved. He opened the bedroom door and walked in, a bounce in his step.

"I come bearing good news," he said, hopping to my side and leaning over the bed. He was—oh God, he was untying me. First my feet, then my wrists. I rolled my wrist, getting the circulation back. He whistled as he undid the last knot. I'd never seen him so… upbeat. I wondered what the news was.

"Put on a dress for me, will you, kitten? Do this one thing for me today." He went to the closet and threw down the remaining dresses that he'd brought for me. "Whichever you want."

I picked up the first dress I saw and a set of lingerie and stood up.

"No! Not in the bathroom. Here. Dress in front of me. You know I can't trust to you do anything without me, kitten."

He watched me carefully as I dressed, his eyes touching me everywhere. I still felt dizzy from the wave of anxiety, but as I dressed I felt better. The one I chose was the red sheath, a shorter dress that hit me just above the knee. He looked me up and down appreciatively and then came over to where I stood.

"Gavriel?"

He kissed me briefly, like he was kissing his wife hello. I didn't know if he was pretending to be happy, or if he actually was happy.

"You look beautiful, dear," he said. "Sit down. Let me brush your hair."

I sat down on the corner of the bed, dazed by his good mood. He retrieved a hairbrush from the bedside drawer and sat behind me. His hands moved through my hair, the brush caressing my scalp gently. There were a lot of knots, but he worked patiently, never yanking the brush. His fingers were long, careful. He would have been a good surgeon, I thought stupidly.

"There," he said. "Now let's go downstairs."

He led me down, his hand guiding me on the small of my back. We passed the statue of horses on the stairs; their eyes seemed to watch me as I went down. When I realized we were heading to the kitchen, I started back in panic.

"It's alright, kitten," he said, catching me against his chest. "You're going to make me something to eat, that's all. That's all."

I trembled and continued. What else could I do?

He sat at the kitchen table, where days earlier I had watched him kill and dismember the professor. He gestured toward the fridge.

"Make us something to eat," he said.

I opened the fridge and looked inside. It felt so weird to look at what a serial killer ate. Everything was so… normal. Milk, eggs, orange juice, shredded cheese.

"What do you want?" I asked.

"Are you good at cooking? No, I don't care. Make us an omelet. You know how to make an omelet, right?"

"Sure."

"There's ham in the bottom shelf."

I took out all of the ingredients and began to do what I had done a million times. Sometimes when I was cooking in someone else's kitchen, I didn't know where anything was, but everything in his place was exactly where I would have put it. Bowls in the side cabinet. A pan underneath the counter next to the stove. I greased the pan with butter and turned the stove to hot. He sat there quietly, watching me as I beat the eggs in a large bowl. Then I took out a knife to cut the ham into pieces. As I finished cutting, I looked up at him. He was watching me intently.

"Did you not want me to use a knife?" I asked.

He raised his eyebrows in a question.

"I—it's a weapon," I said. "I tried to kill you before." As I held the knife in my hand, my palm grew sweaty. I thought about the razor and blinked the thought away.

"Are you going to try to kill me now?" he asked, smiling.

I shook my head. No, I wasn't. I was—I didn't know what I was doing. I put the knife down and sprinkled ham over the cooking eggs in the pan. Added cheese. Flipped the omelet in half, flipped it over to finish cooking.

"Your parents were on the news today," Gav said. "The local station."

I almost knocked the pan off of the stove.

"What—what did they—"

"They thought you had run away again," he said. "They begged for you to not do anything stupid. To come back home."

So nobody was looking for me. Nobody thought I was kidnapped.

As though reading my mind, Gav spoke again.

"Your friend thinks otherwise," he said. "The one with the spiked hair and all the piercings."

"Jules," I murmured. It seemed like so long ago I'd been shelving books alongside her, making jokes about the terrible books people checked out.

"She's the only one who thinks you're kidnapped, though," he said, shrugging. "Nobody will listen to a girl who looks like that."

"Like *what*?"

"You know full well that appearances are all that matter in the world today," he said. "The eggs are done."

So they were. I slid the omelet out onto a plate, cut it in half, made two servings. Gav came around and poured two glasses of orange juice. The silverware clattered onto the table. We sat side by side. I cut my omelet into pieces, holding the knife carefully so that he could see it. He didn't care, or pretended not to.

"Delicious. Wonderful meal." Gav set his knife down onto his plate, crossed over his fork. "What do you want in return?"

I shook my head.

"Nothing, yet."

"You're saving up favors?"

"Maybe." Truth was, I had no idea what I wanted from him. I wanted... I didn't know what I wanted.

"I'll never let you go. If that's what you're waiting for."

"What was the good news?"

"Hmm?"

"You said there was good news. Was it that my parents aren't looking for me?"

"Oh! Oh, no. Although that is good news too. No, I was out looking for the next man to give me some release. A hundred or so miles away from the last victim, so it's perfect. You know, I don't normally kill close to home. This last one was an exception. He was special. That was a mistake, I suppose. It's how you found me, anyway."

"You... you're going to kill someone else?" My mouth dropped open and my fork fell against the plate. I didn't want to eat the last bite of my omelet.

"Yes. Tonight, maybe tomorrow. I've already laid the groundwork. Finding out his schedule, his routine. They always have a routine. You know."

"How—how many people have you killed?"

"A few. One every few months."

"And you get away with it?"

"They rarely get reported as murders, thank God. Most of them are businessmen who have a thousand other secrets - tax evasion, for one. The police usually think they're skipping town to avoid the bills from Uncle Sam. Or if they're in disputes with the local gangs, or if they're addicted to drugs. Lots of evidence pointing in all directions. Except toward me."

"How many?" I wasn't sure I even wanted to know, but my curiosity got the best of me.

"Are you going to finish that?" Gav reached over and forked the last piece of my omelet into his mouth. "You know, psychopaths really aren't that dangerous."

"Really." I frowned. He was acting like it wasn't a big deal. And he seemed so normal now, in the daylight. It made me feel sick. Sick that I had been falling for him, sick that even now, I didn't know if I hated him or if I was pretending to hate him.

"It's only around three percent of all violent crimes that are committed by psychopaths, you know." He chewed on one side of his mouth thoughtfully. "The vast majority of murders are done by irate spouses, or gangs, or whatever. Not by people like me."

"I'm sure that's a relief to all the people you kill."

"No, I suppose not. But everybody always worries about the psychopaths coming after them, and never about the wife they're cheating on, or their drug dealers, or their disgruntled employees. It's just not *likely* for a serial killer to get you."

"You got me."

"Not like that, kitten," Gav said, chuckling.

"Don't kill him today."

He swallowed. The smile faded from his face.

"Excuse me?"

"You asked what I wanted. Another trade, right? I want you to not kill him."

"You don't know this man," Gav said, his lips pressed together so hard that they were turning white.

"He was convicted of spousal abuse two years ago and bought the judge. All he had to do was pay a fine and attend some bullshit counseling sessions. He's been fucking his intern—"

"I don't care," I said, my voice shaking. "Don't kill him. Don't leave me again today. Don't do it."

"Kitten—"

"You asked what I want. That's what I want."

Anger clouded his face. He stood and picked up my plate, stacked it atop his, and dropped both of them into the sink. My shoulders jerked at the noise.

"Upstairs."

He grabbed me by the wrist and dragged me out of the kitchen. His face was dark, as dark as it had been after I'd tried to kill him with the razor. He pulled me back up the stairs and into the bedroom. My heart was racing. What had I done?

"Lay down."

I sat on the bed, but I wasn't quick enough. He shoved me down and looped the rope around my wrists.

"Gav, you promised—"

"You're hurting me with this."

"But you promised—"

"For today. Yes. I won't kill him today. There's your trade." He spat the words bitterly as he tied my ankles roughly, not caring how tight they were.

"Where are you going?"

"What does it matter to you?"

"Don't lie to me." I thought of my parents, about them asking me to come home. I didn't have a home. I never had a home, not with them, not with anybody. And not here.

"I'll be back soon," he said.

"Gav, don't kill him! Don't kill anyone, don't—"

But he was already gone.

Gav

The shadow taunted me. I could go anyway, lie to her and go for the kill. It was a man who deserved to die, and I did not deserve to be like this. The shadow clouded all of my vision as I banged down the stairs, got the ax out from the hallway closet. I slammed the door shut behind me.

In the forest, the birds stopped chirping as I walked into the clearing. I dragged a small fallen tree over to the chopping block, hacked it into logs. Put the first log up onto the block.

"Trade. This isn't a trade."

My arms swung the ax. The blade arced up and then down, splintering the log into two pieces. The noise shattered the silence of the forest and I heard the birds flying off their perches. I replaced the log and swung again.

"This is revenge. This is her teasing me. Stupid. I could kill her if I wanted to."

I could pretend that my anger was due to injustice. That I wanted to kill this man to save the people around him. But there was no saving anyone in this world, and all I wanted was for the damn shadow to go away.

Splinters rained down. Like bones splintering. I

imagined my next victim on the chopping block, pleading for his life. Rage boiled up inside of me and I raised the ax, brought it down with such force that it stuck in the block. I put my foot up against the log and rocked the handle until the ax came loose again.

The logs went quickly. I chopped and chopped until the muscles in my arms ached and there was nothing left to split. The world was almost completely black, the shadow taking me over with a desire for relief. Cutting wood was no solution. I gathered the chopped logs in my arms, piled them up near the house in a dozen trips. Overloading myself each time. I could feel my back already beginning to hurt from the weight of carrying so much. Good. The pain would drive the shadow back, maybe. Give me something else to focus on.

Back in the house, up the stairs. In bed I found her tied up, her neck pale and tempting. The walls dripped with shadow and I clenched my fists, trying not to kill her.

She looked terrified as I came forward, stripping off my shirt. This was her choice, her decision.

"Gavriel?"

Her voice echoed in my brain, pinging back and forth inside. Was that who I was? A killer? A psychopath? What did she want to make of me? I bent my head to hers and saw my reflection in her eyes. A murderer, yes. Not today, though.

"You wanted me before, kitten. I hope you want me now." My hands went to my pants, where I was already hard. Wanting her. Needing her. If I couldn't have the release I sorely needed, I would have to distract myself elsewhere.

"Gav—"

"You don't want me to kill him?" I hissed. "Fine. But I'm going to do whatever I want to you."

CHAPTER EIGHTEEN

Kat

"This is your choice," he said, dropping his underwear on the ground next to the bed. "You understand the decision you've made?"

I looked up at him. He scowled down at me, looking angry for disrupting for his plan. And looking... scared?

"Gav—"

"Tell me to go and I'll go. Anytime. Understand?"

I nodded mutely. He stood at the bedside, his cock twitching, half-erect. I hadn't seen him in full light before, but looking at him now I wondered if I would be able to take him inside of me. He was huge. I felt something inside me twist in painful desire.

"What do you want?" he asked.

I swallowed, knowing everything he was asking. Knowing what he really wanted. I couldn't give it to him, but I could give something else.

"I want you," I said.

It was coercion, I told myself. It was all a lie, all of this.

But it was none of that, not really. I hated the man he wanted to kill, hated that man more than I hated my kidnapper. In my mind, the face of the man he had gone to kill was my stepfather's face. I knew what those men were like. I hated them.

Was I saving that man, an abuser? Or was I doing this to satisfy myself? Or both?

Gav was rougher this time. He did not waste a second on foreplay. Instead he swung a leg over me and straddled my chest.

Oh god. Oh god.

His cock hung in front of me. Long, thick, the skin smooth. The foreskin was already pulled back by the tension of his erection, exposing the pink mushroom tip.

"Tell me, kitten, have you ever been in this position before?"

"No," I said honestly. The few guys I'd ever been with had been younger. All they knew was missionary position, and the only blow jobs I'd given had happened on couches, in dorm rooms, after parties where I'd had enough beer to dull my senses. I barely remembered what I'd done to get them off.

I breathed in, trying to slow down my pounding heart. What if he didn't like what I did? Would he hurt me?

He pulled a pillow down and lifted my head to sneak it under me. All the while, I couldn't take my eyes off of his cock. It twitched with his heartbeat at random times, and when he reached for the pillow it swung up, grazing my cheek.

"If you try anything to hurt me, I'll kill you," he said. "I'm being nice, kitten. I could just leave you here and go get my release elsewhere."

"No," I whispered, thinking of the man on the table, the knife dripping with blood. "Don't. Please don't."

"Then make me want to stay here with you."

With that, he cupped his hand around the back of my head and lifted me slightly. He slid his cock into my mouth and I panicked. Gagging, I coughed and jerked my head back. I looked up, worried, but he was smiling.

"Relax your tongue, kitten," he said.

I did what he said, and when he put his cock into my mouth again it slid in smoothly. As he thrust farther in, the tip of his cock hit the back of my throat. My eyes watered but I kept my tongue down.

"Ohhh," he moaned.

I might have thought that he was faking, but his cock, already stiff, hardened and grew in my mouth. He slid himself out, and I let my lips cover his head as he rocked out of me just barely, then rocked back in.

The hand that he used to steady the back of my head spread out, his fingers twining through my hair. It felt like when he was giving me a shampoo, a gentle caress completely at odds with the hard cock that slid forward and filled my mouth. I whimpered when he thrust too far, and he grinned as he pulled out.

He took his cock in his hand and let the tip touch my lips, the sticky precum mixing with the saliva on my already moistened lips. I breathed in and could feel him tense as the cool air moved over his cock.

"Easy, now. You're doing so well. Suck the tip, kitten."

I accepted his cock eagerly, knowing now that I wouldn't be gagged. I closed my eyes and moved my tongue in circles over his smooth skin. Trying to remember all of the tips I'd read in my sister's dumb Cosmo magazines. *Flick the tongue against the tip. Make a seal with your lips around the whole head and suck. Breathe through your nose.* My tongue was starting to hurt.

"Kitten."

I opened my eyes and looked up to see him frowning at me. My heart sank.

"What are you doing?"

"I—I'm trying…"

"Pretend that it's me licking you," he said sternly. "What do you want me to do to you?"

Everything. The word died in my mouth. Instead of letting me talk, he slid his cock back into my mouth.

Yes. What he would do to me. I closed my eyes again, thinking of how he'd teased me. How he'd tormented me. I let my tongue slide out, exploring the circumference of his thick cock. When I touched the bottom of his head with the tip of my tongue, I felt him tense up and gasp above me.

There. I pressed my tongue to the base of his head. There was a ridge, bumped underneath, and I slid my mouth down to that place, sucking hard, letting my tongue flick out again and again. I traced the ridge, following it in a circle. Letting it take me wherever it wanted to go. Soft kisses on the fleshy part of the tip, breaths to cool him down, then back to kissing.

I wanted him so badly now. Thinking about his tongue down between my thighs, doing what I was doing, I twisted with desire. My body was already hot under the dress, and I wondered if he would take it off when I was done, if he would take me. I sucked harder, the way I imagined he would, and it made him groan above me.

His weight shifted forward and I took him into me

farther, letting my tongue slip down to the base of his cock. My throat jerked at the touch of his cock when he was so far in, but I forced my body to relax, to take him farther. He moaned and moaned. Tied up, I couldn't touch myself, but I was getting so turned on by listening to his responses that I thought I could come in an instant if he'd touch me there, even once.

On top of me, he began to rock. I felt the rhythm that he wanted and matched it. His hand supported my neck, and I relaxed into his grip, letting him slide into me as far as he wanted, my tongue lapping at the base of his cock each time he withdrew. His fingers were hot and damp with sweat, and I could feel him grow hotter against my chest as well, even through the dress.

My legs were tied apart, and it killed me to not be able to push my thighs together, to have any pressure down there. His thick hard cock moved faster and faster and all I could think about was how I wanted him down between my legs, how I wanted his tongue, his cock inside of me. I moaned along with him and felt his shivers as my mouth trembled against him. My lips gripped him tightly, sucking and licking at the same time. This, this was what I wanted. Yes, this. This—

"Kitten," he moaned hoarsely. My eyes had been closed, but I opened them just in time to see him look down at me, his eyebrows turned up in the middle, as though pleading me to continue. "I... I..."

I knew what he was unable to say, and I tilted my head forward to take him completely inside of me. His cock stiffened, the base growing impossibly hard under my lips, and his seed came hot and spurting against my tongue. I swallowed reflexively to keep from gagging, his salty taste filling my mouth, and swallowed again until there was nothing left. I continued to suck and lick, more softly, the way I imagined I'd want to be licked after an orgasm.

He withdrew quickly, and the room turned cool as he swung his leg off of me and released me from his weight. He sat on the edge of the bed, and I twisted my neck to watch him pull on his underwear. Bent over, his head resting slightly on the tips of his fingers, he looked almost as though he was praying.

I burned for relief. There was no way he could stop now. I felt as though he'd done to me all of the things I'd done to him, but I was only on the verge of climax.

"Gav?"

He did not turn. He made no motion at all to let me know that he had heard me. I tried a bit louder.

"Gav?"

"What is it?"

"I—I mean—would you—can you do that for me?"

As soon as I asked, I knew he would deny me. But I was taken aback at his reaction. Not angry, no. He wasn't angry at all. Instead, he began to laugh. Softly, at first, then louder and louder, until I worried that he was truly insane. More insane than I'd thought before.

His head snapped toward me, cutting off his laugh abruptly.

"You want more, kitten?"

My mouth was dry.

"I need it. Gavriel, please, I want it so badly. You don't know—"

"I know it quite well," he said brusquely. He stood up, and I saw his eyes flatten, cover his emotions.

"You're the one who doesn't know."

He walked to the bathroom door and I nearly screamed.

"Just touch me, just a bit," I begged, hating myself for being so weak. "It won't take long, I'm almost there."

"No, kitten," he said. "Your decision, your choice. It's a trade, of course. Always a trade."

I bit my lip.

"I gave you what you wanted—" I started to say, but his dark look cut my words off on my tongue.

"No," he said. "I've already given you what you asked for. Now you'll see a bit of what I have to face each day."

He paused, and looked down at me with pity in his eyes.

"I don't get to kill, and you don't get to come."

Gav

Breathe in, breathe out. Water splashed on my face, cooled my heated skin.

I couldn't believe what she was making me do. The shadow left me alone for a moment, but as soon as I left her side it was back, sliding in at the corners, uncurling its tendrils around my center of vision.

She'd saved the man for one day, that was all. If I wanted to, I could kill him tomorrow. The thought calmed me somewhat. Imagining the man on my table, my knife slicing down through the layers of skin and muscle and fat. Exposing his insides to the air. Blood isn't red until it meets the oxygen in the atmosphere, and then it changes color instantly.

Yes, I could kill him later. It soothed me, and I played out his death in my mind like a tape, rewinding, replaying, changing parts around. Would I cut off his fingers first? That sometimes made it better, to hear their screams as I popped the joints one by one. Fingers weren't lethal, and I could keep him conscious throughout. Yes, that's what I would do.

I returned to the bedroom in a better mood. She lay staring at the ceiling and would not look at me when I came and sat beside her.

"I'm going out for the afternoon," I said.

She whipped her head back towards me.

"You said—"

"I won't kill him today. We made a trade."

"A trade." She whispered it.

"Not sure if it was worth it? Well, kitten, you can always change your mind."

"No."

"I'll bring you back a present. No trades, just a gift."

"Untie my hand, please," she said. "One hand, that's all I need. That's all I—"

"Later," I said. "But not when I'm gone. I can't leave you untied. Surely you understand that."

The rejection rippled through her body. I put my hand on her stomach and she winced.

"Don't," she whispered. "Not if you're going to leave me."

I lifted my hand away from her.

"I'll be back," I said. "And... thank you."

She looked up at me, confusion quirking her beautiful arched eyebrows.

"For giving me a measure of relief. It's not enough, not for me, but you tried. I—thank you."

I turned and left before she could respond.

CHAPTER NINETEEN

Kat

He came back later and threw a few books down next to me on the bed. Then untied my hands and feet. An hour earlier, I would have been ready to throw myself at him in a desperate attempt for either an orgasm or an escape, but I had calmed down a lot since then.

He had, too, it seemed. He smiled comfortingly at me.

It was his *thank you* that had really made me look at him differently. Strange that such a little thing could make me feel so much better. But I felt that I'd given something to him that he couldn't take himself. In a way, he needed me.

That was good and bad at the same time. There was no way he would ever let me go, but maybe I could convince him slowly to give me more space. More freedom. And then—

Then what? I couldn't risk trying to kill him again. I would take it slowly, I decided, rubbing my wrists. Try to gain his confidence back. Then I could decide on my next move.

I picked up one of the books. *The Billionaire's Courtesan.* The cover was one of those pink and gold numbers with raised lettering. I always wondered why they didn't do the bumpy lettering over the woman's breasts. It would be a heaving bosom. Get it?

Yeah, I didn't make myself laugh, either.

"I thought you might like these," Gav said.

"Romance novels?" I tossed the book down and looked at the others. *The Cowboy and the Bride. Her Last Virgin Night.*

"There was one on your cart when we first met."

"That's… sweet of you." I picked up the cowboy one and rifled through the pages. The second chapter started with him "*exposing his throbbing member*" and only got worse. I giggled, cupping my hand over my mouth. The word *member* seemed so funny at that moment that I had to suppress a burst of laughter.

"You don't like them?"

"No, it's just...We make fun of these."

"We?"

"Jules and I. My friend, the one that was there. She called you Fabio afterward, because of how you looked."

"Oh? How did I look? I don't have that stunning long blond hair."

I looked up at Gavriel as he sat down next to me. I didn't know if it was because he'd untied me, or because I'd finally gotten him off, but I felt like we were having a normal conversation for the first time. It was weirder than any other conversation we'd had, strangely enough. Like we'd known each other for longer than we actually had.

"Come on. You know how you look."

"Well-groomed?"

"Attractive. Much hotter than any guy that normally comes into the library, that's for damn sure."

He laughed. With the early afternoon light coming

in through the window, the room felt cozy. Romantic. If I hadn't known that I had just been bound up on the bed, thinking this man was going to kill me, I wouldn't have believed it myself.

"I don't think I could be on the cover of a romance novel."

"I think you could." I flopped down on my back and let my eyes skim over the pages without reading anything. "That could be your new career."

"Stop killing people and start ravishing virgins?"

"Sure, why not?" We were *flirting*. This was so weird.

"I only picked up one virgin book, but there were dozens of them on the shelf. What is it about romance novels where the heroine has to be a virgin?"

"Easy. She has to be perfect," I said. "Or at least perfectly innocent. The heroes too."

"Mmm?"

"That's the thing about the heroes in these kinds of books - they're always so perfect. Perfect looks, lots of money, super confident, huge cocks. They're book boyfriends."

"Book boyfriends?"

"You've never heard of that? Like, if you really like a guy from a book, if you're totally obsessed with him. You pretend he's your book boyfriend. It's a way to imagine yourself dating a charming billionaire."

"I kill billionaires. They're usually horrible people."

"Come on, Fabio." I swatted him with the paperback. At least he was talking about killing other people and not me.

"My name is Gavriel."

"Super hot, super rich, super big cock. You don't think you'd make a good book boyfriend?"

"I'm not a goddamn book boyfriend." His words were flat, and although his mouth was curved, the smile didn't reach his eyes. He'd lost the flirtatious manner he had when he walked in.

"No?"

Gav stood up and walked to the window. I thought he would just ignore me, but then he spoke again. His voice was lower, more serious. His long fingers tapped the windowsill as he spoke.

"I kill your book boyfriends. Your billionaires, your CEOs. I carve them limb from limb and destroy the evidence. Nobody could ever mistake me for a hero."

"No. No, I suppose not." I licked my lips. I didn't know what to say. "Thanks anyway. For the books."

He turned back to me, his face pleasant and inviting again. The light pouring in through the window illuminated his front, shone through his white shirt and gave him a halo around his dark hair. He was wrong. Standing there, all smooth planes and hard lines of muscle, he looked exactly like a hero. But I knew better.

"Aren't you going to use them to pleasure yourself?" he asked.

"What, the books? Like, right now?"

"Yes."

An idea sparked in my mind and made it to my tongue before I spent any time thinking about it.

"Do you want me to?"

"Yes."

"A trade?"

He smiled.

"You know me too well, kitten. What do you want from this trade?"

That was easy. There was one thing I'd been dreaming about for all the hours he had me locked up in the basement, for all the hours he had me tied up to his bedposts.

"Take me outside."

His eyes flashed dangerously as he leaned against the wall and crossed his arms.

"Outside?"

"Just for a little walk. My legs are so cramped from staying inside."

He thought for a moment, one hand stroking his chin where his black stubble had been growing like a lawn after the spring's first rainstorm. Such a liar. He would be perfect on a cover. *The Pirate Rogue*, I thought to myself. *The Handsome Killer*.

"Yes. That's a fair trade."

He sat down in the arm chair next to the bed and motioned to the books.

"Well?"

My heart skipped a beat.

"Are you going to stay and watch?"

"Of course. This is a trade, after all. How could I be sure you'd truly pleasured yourself unless I was a witness?"

I blushed, then cursed myself for blushing. God, here I was with a murderer, a serial killer, someone who I'd tried to kill, and I was embarrassed to have him watch me get myself off while reading a romance novel. Some things just don't make sense.

"I'm not really in the mood right now," I said.

"That's what the books are for."

I swallowed the lump in my throat. I was about to speak again but then he cut me off.

"We can stay here for a while. Until you're ready. I've already been outside once today." So nonchalant. Such an asshole.

In the window beyond his chair, the pine branches beckoned.

"Fine," I said. It wasn't fine, but it would have to be. I really did want to go outside. For one, I wanted to see what the house looked like underneath the windows, if there was a possible escape route from the bedroom. And for two... well, I hadn't been outside in days.

I shoved the pillows up to the top of the bed and lay back, propping my elbows on my knees. Picking up *The Cowboy and the Bride*, I began to read.

Gav

At first, I could tell she was nervous. The book's pages flipped rapidly, and I saw her cheeks flush pink. One hand rested on her knee, and the other held the book open, creasing the well-worn spine. How many women had held that book this way, I wondered?

None so beautiful as her. Her hand was soft with curves, her fingernails clipped sensibly. I longed to see her touch herself. Page after page turned, and nothing.

"Are you not used to having someone watch you, kitten?"

She flushed harder. God, her lips were delicious when she bit them slightly, the pucker of her cheeks as she got mad.

"I… I've never. Not with someone watching."

"Take your time, then."

"I was, thanks." Her sarcasm was clipped and she raised the book to hide her face.

But then, oh then—her hand moved down, under the hem of her dress. I saw the fabric slide up over her creamy thighs, the sweet pink silk of her panties revealed inch by inch. Her fingers grazed the fabric just over her sweet slit.

I'd tasted her there, and the memory of her delicious flesh aroused me instantly. It's true, we men are visual creatures. I wanted to watch her, every piece of her, as she touched herself. Thankfully, the book slipped lower and I could see her nose peeking over the cover, then her mouth. Her perfect pink heart of a mouth, almost as tasty as the lips between her thighs.

Her fingers stroked slowly, patiently. So patient. The sensation must be barely there. I could see between her legs the fabric darkening, turning wet. Her eyes softened, her eyelids drooping down at the corners as she continued reading, continued stroking.

Shifting in my seat, I was not prepared for the small gasp that came from her as she found herself. Such a slight squeak of pleasure, and yet it caused a rush of lustful thoughts to come over me. I was hard, getting harder with every small whispering breath of hers, and I couldn't help but stroke myself with the back of my knuckles, as though smoothing out the fabric of my pants.

"Are you touching yourself over there?" Her voice had a hitch in it, but it was teasing, playful.

"Why did you think I wanted to watch you?"

Her eyebrows raised, and just as quickly settled back down as her eyes moved over another paragraph. Her fingers pressed harder, squeezing from both sides through her panties. She turned the page with her thumb, expertly. So she *had* done this before, just not with an audience.

I unzipped my pants. She moaned, and my cock twitched. I imagined myself between those legs. She was mine, mine and nobody else's, but I admit that I couldn't help but feel jealous that it was not me who was arousing her, not me teasing her to the edge. My hand gripped my cock. Most women I took home couldn't wait to jump into bed with me. This was... different.

Good, but different.

Kat

The words on the page swam before my eyes. I'd gotten as far as the first hayloft scene, where the cowboy had realized that his bride was, surprise, surprise, a virgin. Then he'd gone down on her, and I'd stopped imagining a cowboy.

My eyelashes fluttered as I moved my hand between my thighs. I could feel myself starting to get wet as I read along, but I wasn't reading the words anymore. There wasn't a cowboy in my mind, no virgin bride rolling around on the hay. I was imagining Gavriel.

I tried to bring my thoughts back to the book at hand, but it was no use once he started touching himself. I turned the pages and tried to avoid looking directly at him sitting over there in the chair. He'd pulled out his cock and was stroking it slowly, easily. I watched the foreskin sliding up over his head, then back down, his hand tightening at the base.

It was true - I'd never had a guy watch me masturbate before. But also, I'd never watched a guy jack off. I mean, I'd seen clips from comedies where they did it - the classic bathroom scene in *Something About Mary*. But never for real. No guy had ever masturbated in my presence, let alone while watching me. The strangest part of it was how much it turned me on, to see his long fingers wrapped entirely around his erection.

His breath caught in his throat, and I found myself catching my own breath, matching him. He'd closed his eyes, tilting his head back onto the armchair. I let my book drop, watching him move his hand over his long shaft. His thumb flicked the tip at the end of every stroke. His rhythm became mine, and as the pressure grew inside of me, I stopped pretending to read.

My hand moved faster and faster, harder and harder, and I watched him, stroke after stroke, his cock growing harder and bigger in his hand. God, his lips. Those lips, touching me between my legs, his tongue inside of me... I rubbed furiously, trying to get to the point of release. I needed it, needed to get rid of all these thoughts about him.

Then he lifted his head, and his eyes locked onto

mine.

My mouth dropped open in shock, my hand still moving as the ache inside me grew insistently. The book lay limp and discarded on the sheets next to me. There was no pretending that I wasn't looking at him. To my surprise, he licked his lips but said nothing.

I whimpered, my eyes fluttering shut. I needed this. I needed to get rid of this ache. The sunlight in the room shone red through my closed eyelids. I worked my hand against my swollen clit, my fingers tense and hard. Like he had been hard against me. I wanted so desperately to open my eyes, to look at him. My heart was pumping hard, the pressure of my climax rising and rising inside of me.

No.

I rolled over onto my side, trying to get a better angle. My hand was squeezed tight between my thighs, and I rocked against my fingers, trying hard to push myself. My other hand clenched the sheets, my fingers curled into a fist.

"Kitten."

I opened my eyes to find him standing next to the bed, his hand gripping his cock hard in one fist. His eyes were full of desire. I whimpered. I didn't want to ask him for anything, didn't want anything from him. Or did I?

He knelt down on the bed and lay next to me. His eyes asked permission and I granted it. Our faces were so close that we shared a breath, and I was still rocking, rocking against my fingers. I moaned. Every part of me ached for release, but my climax seemed to never want to come.

His free hand came up and covered my clenched fist and I abandoned the sheets for his palm. His fingers twined around mine, his palm hot against my own. The bed moved with his rhythm, now, too, his hand moving as fast as mine down where I dared not look.

At his touch, my body arched hard against the bed. I felt the pressure rise inside my body, come close to bursting. Sweat beaded his dark upper lip. I stared at his face, those dark features, those light eyes, and all the while I rocked in rhythm against my hand, pushing harder, harder—

A look in his eyes. That was what did it. As he stroked himself, I could see the tension in every muscle of his mouth, in every twitch of his eyebrows. It heightened every little bit of arousal in my own body, sending my nerves into a deep shiver whenever he twitched. Then he moaned and his eyes went soft, deep, losing themselves as they stared into my face.

His moan was a low rumble, and I felt the shudder of it send me over the edge. My hips pushed forward and my fingers squeezed and he squeezed back and I came hard, god, so hard, the orgasm bursting forth into a low scream that I buried into the pillow. My fingers pressed deep into me as I shuddered over and over again, my body rippling with relief.

His breath caught, and I looked down to see him grip himself tight and with one thrust end it. He spurted between his fingers, his lips parting in a silent groan of ecstasy, his seed soaking the sheets between us.

Then his head fell back next to mine on the pillow and he gazed into my eyes and I could not look away, the same way a rabbit cannot tear its eyes from the owl hunting it. He licked his lips and I tried to catch my breath, my pulse pounding in my ears.

When I finally looked down, I was still holding his hand.

CHAPTER TWENTY

Kat

He let go of my hand and got up first, tucking away his softening cock and zipping his pants back up. I was still shivering from the force of my orgasm.

"Let's go."

"Go?" A whisper. I could barely talk.

"Outside. That was the trade, wasn't it?"

Oh, right. The trade.

"If your legs can work properly, that is."

"I'm fine."

I struggled to my feet and followed him shakily downstairs. I'd never masturbated next to someone before. It wasn't sex - not exactly. It had felt, impossibly, *more* intimate than sex. It had been a release of sorts, but there was no way I could ever have come to such a blindingly strong orgasm on my own.

Everything around me seemed different.

Gav was different, too. When he touched me to guide me through the house the way he normally did, his hand felt gentle on my back, not forceful. I found myself wobbling down the steps and toward the front door, but he had my arm every step of the way, supporting me.

Such a strange intimacy.

We came to the front door. I stopped in my tracks, but he opened the door as nonchalantly as though it was an everyday occurrence. Which, for him, I suppose it was.

"Did you need shoes?"

I had forgotten my feet were bare. I shook my head no. I wanted to get outside. I *needed* to get outside.

"It should be fine," he said, more to himself than to me. "It's grassy outside."

I walked forward past the threshold of the door, my knees trembling. My stomach was tight across my pelvis. Unwilling to believe this was possible, I kept expecting to run into an invisible wall just outside the door. But no, I was out of the house and then he was leading me forward. The wood planks of the front steps were rough under my feet, warm from the afternoon sun.

With my hand on his arm, we walked down the steps and out into the world.

It was spring, and it was a beautiful day outside. I stopped a few feet away from the house, tilting my head back. The sun was so bright that it made my eyes water, and the warmth caressed my skin.

"We'll go this way," Gavriel said, motioning towards the woods. "The path is nearly all grass."

We walked across the driveway toward the pines. Under my toes, the asphalt was dark and hot, and I walked a bit faster to not burn the soles of my feet. I loved the feeling, though, I loved the prickling sensation. A breeze sent goosebumps running along my arms, but then the sun warmed them back up as soon as the wind died down.

Another sharp breeze sent the pines above us shuddering, and pollen rained down, blown sideways by the wind. The sun glittered off of the golden pinpricks, making the air seem like an ethereal galaxy of dust. If I had allergies, I'd be horrified - my old roommate had hated pollen and refused to go outside in the spring. But I was mesmerized.

We walked slowly. The path was only wide enough for one person, and Gav let me walk ahead of him. My eyes darted from one treasure to another. The amber resin glowing like gemstones in the cracks of the pine branches. The bright yellow ovals of fungus growing on logs, their edges wrinkled and neon. I let my hand trail down the rough bark of a redwood, my fingertips touching every crack and crevice. A line of ants curved around the trunk, and as I stopped and watched, I could see the whole tree's surface *moving* with activity.

At my feet, something moved, and I jumped back, startled, right into Gavriel's arms. He waited for me to find my balance, then dropped his hands away.

"It's just a newt."

"A what?"

Gavriel bent down to pick up the wriggling creature.

"They're everywhere out here, especially after a rain. Be careful you don't step on them. They usually don't start moving until you come too close."

"He's a cutie. Hey, cutie."

"Want to hold him?"

Gav held the newt out to me, daring me with his eyebrows to take it. Boldly, I reached out and he dropped the little animal into my hand.

Immediately it began to wiggle around. I held it in my hand, my thumb pressed lightly on its back to keep it from wriggling out of my grasp. Its skin was nearly translucent, and I could feel its belly rise and fall against my palm. Its little feet were wet against my skin.

"Looks like you found yourself a pet."

"Slimy," I said. "Not the best pet to cuddle with."

"Better than a banana slug."

I laughed and crouched down, letting the little newt crawl off of my hand. It flopped belly-first into the wet leaves and kept wriggling away.

"Be free, little newt!"

"So much for a pet."

"He can still be my pet. I'll come back and bring it some… what do newts eat, anyway?"

"Insects?" Gav shrugged.

"Yuck. Well, never mind that, then."

We kept walking, me in front. On the sides of the path, I noticed all of the little newts I'd never noticed before. And I was careful not to step on any of them.

It was so weird. I'd spent every day for the past three years walking through the arboretum on my way to work, but I'd never noticed anything about the trees there. Here, though, it was like every new tree had something amazing about it - the curve of the branches, the way the leaves fluttered like clusters of green wings on the ends of their twigs.

I stopped in the middle of a clearing, and Gav's footsteps stopped behind me. In front of us, a massive redwood stretched up to the sky. I tilted my head back and looked up at the tree. The bark smelled so good, damp and fragrant, and the only sound was the rustle of the pines around us.

Why had I never noticed how beautiful they were before?

I began to cry. I didn't know why - I wasn't sad. On the contrary, the huge tree in front of me filled my heart with joy, so much that I felt incapable of holding it all in. I was outside, I was free if only for a moment, and this tree stretched out above me, making the whole world of humans seem utterly ridiculous and insignificant.

Gav didn't try to comfort me. He didn't touch me, and we walked in silence the whole way back to the house. I felt so calm, as though nothing mattered, not even the mess I'd created for myself. Nothing mattered, because those trees would keep on growing forever, long after I was dead and gone. They would keep being beautiful.

At the front door, I paused and turned to look back once at the waving pines. He held the door open for me patiently.

I looked up at him. His eyes were calm like the ocean. I didn't know how to tell him that he'd given me the best present I'd ever received. I didn't know how to tell him what I'd realized.

Instead, I leaned forward on tiptoe and kissed him gently on the lips.

The first time I'd kissed him, he had kissed me back deeply. This time, though, he let me guide the kiss, and when I stepped back he didn't press any farther.

"Thank you," I whispered, and went inside.

Gav

What was she doing to me, this girl? I did not know whether to trust her when she kissed me. My plan had been to seduce her, but now that it seemed to be happening I was completely lost. I didn't like how it made me feel - like I cared whether or not her feelings for me were real.

That night, she made dinner and I poured us both glasses of wine. She smiled brightly and drank, and we talked the way I imagine normal people talk. She asked to go upstairs and read, and I let her go without following her. The kitchen seemed so empty without her there.

Afterward, I went for a walk. Outside, the stars shone. I liked it out here, far away from the city. The bright pinpricks of light were brighter, here. They drove away the shadow.

She had driven away the shadow, too, though. On our walk, I'd seen the world through her eyes, and the shadow hadn't come back, not even afterward, not until later when I'd left her alone.

No. I couldn't become dependent on her for that. I had never been dependent on anyone.

But she is yours, my mind said. _To do with as you want._

The reminder only made the hurt worse. I did not want to force her to love me. Even this deception... it made my stomach twist in a strange way. Whenever people talked about feeling guilty, this was what I imagined they felt. The twisting inside, the tightness in the chest. I had never felt it before, and I did not want to feel it now.

The shadow fluttered at the edges of my mind, but she was more of a distraction to me now.

I went back inside. She was asleep, a book fallen half-finished by her side. I replaced the bookmark and lay down next to her sleeping body. I would not wake her up to tie her wrists to the bedposts. Not tonight. She looked so peaceful.

Maybe in the morning, before I left to go make my visit.

I put an arm around her protectively. To protect her, or to protect me? I did not know the answer to that question anymore.

CHAPTER TWENTY-ONE

Kat

Gav was right about one thing - his wine selection was incredible. The Syrah he'd picked out for dinner had paired perfectly with the steak, and I'd drunk two full glasses before I realized it. He only smiled and flooded my glass again, and the smile made my heart skip a beat.

I was sure that he wanted to get me drunk to do… whatever it was he wanted to do to me. But when I'd asked, he let me go back upstairs to read and left me alone for hours. Strange. He was so strange. And the wine had made me so sleepy. I passed out before he came upstairs.

When I woke up the next morning, he was nowhere to be seen. The room was dim; facing west, the sun's light wouldn't come in until the afternoon. Only a thin gray light illuminated the walls. And my hands were tied up to the bedposts with the same red rope as before. My ankles were free, though.

My pulse pounded. What had he done to me?

Looking down frantically, I saw that I was dressed the same way I had been last night. My underwear was still on, and from what I could tell, he hadn't touched me at all.

Why?

Although it should have made me feel better, this

realization actually shot panic through my system. It was strange that he had gotten me drunk and then tied me up and then done... nothing. I didn't know if I'd wanted him to or not. But that he hadn't bothered to wake me up disturbed me for a reason I couldn't put my finger on.

"Gav?"

I waited to make sure he wasn't just in the bathroom, but there was no response.

The bathroom. I had to go to the bathroom. As soon as I realized it, the urge to pee hit me even harder. I'd drunk way too much wine last night, and if he wasn't around to let me out, I was going to pee the bed.

I yelled a bit louder, to carry my voice downstairs. Surely he wouldn't have left me tied up without letting me go to the bathroom.

"Gav!"

Nothing.

I twisted my body, curling my body close together. My feet could reach the knots if I stretched, I bet. I could even escape, if he was gone. Maybe he was gone. But where would he—

Oh, shit.

My mind focused in an instant. Yesterday, the only thing stopping him from killing that man had been the trade. But today—

No, he wouldn't.

Of course he would. He was a killer.

"GAV!" I screamed at the top of my lungs, and my dry throat ached with the strain of the shouting. I didn't care. *"GAV!"*

I had to get out. Sure, I had to get to the bathroom, but more than that, I had to stop him from killing another person. If he was gone, he would be driving over to wherever he'd said he'd found the next victim. As I thought about it, I realized that I wasn't scared for his next victim. I was scared for him.

Where had he gone? I racked my brain even as I twisted my body up, trying to get my feet to reach the knot. He'd said a hundred miles away. That means I had time, if he had left not too long ago. But how could I know?

My toes touched the rope, and I curled them around the top of the knot, trying to get a grip. My neck was bent at a weird angle, and I had to pee, oh god, I had to pee so bad.

I had to get out. My toes slipped off of the rope, and a shooting pain crossed my abs. I nearly cried out loud. Trying to keep myself from peeing was too much in this position.

But I couldn't let him do it. I couldn't let him kill.

"GAV!" I screamed. My chest began to tighten.

No. Not a panic attack. Not now.

"No," I said to myself, as I gasped for breath. "*No, no, no, no!*"

Anxiety gripped my throat so hard that I thought my windpipe had collapsed. I didn't have my pills. If I had my pills, I would be fine. But no pills. No way to move, to sit up. My arms were stretched out to the sides, and I couldn't relax.

"GAAAAAAAV!"

God, I had to pee. Oh god, I had to pee. It was going to come out if he didn't show up... *now.* I clenched my thighs together and tried to hold it. The tenseness in my chest grew. Was I having a heart attack?

Jesus, what would happen to me if I had a heart attack?

It wasn't a heart attack. It wasn't a heart attack.

"Breathe, Kat," I repeated, my belly full and tight and needing release. "Deep breaths. In, out." I couldn't breathe deeply, not with my bladder so full. It was no use. I had to try to get out of this bed, no matter what.

I twisted my legs up above my head again, and again my toes slipped. This time my leg fell down, and I couldn't stop myself. My body was too tense, and I had to let go.

Warmth spread as I pissed myself. I moaned, trying to shift my body over to the side of the bed, but it was no use. I soaked through my underwear, my dress, the sheets. The pungent odor of urine rose from below, stinging my nose.

Tears filled my eyes as I gasped for air. The humiliation was enough to make me cry, but apart from that I was no closer to escaping, to preventing Gav from bringing another man back here to kill him.

He would stick him with a needle, just like the other man.

Breathe, Kat. I sucked in air, but it wasn't enough. The whole room seemed to close in on me, fuzzy and dark. I twisted my leg up again, but I couldn't even see the ties around my wrists.

He would tie the man down on the table, tighten the straps.

No, Kat. No.

I shook my head and clenched my eyes shut, breathing through my teeth. My teeth were hurting from my jaw being clenched so tight. The wetness on my lower half turned cold in the air as I twisted up, trying to find the knot with my toes. If only I had a knife...

He had a knife. He would cut the man open.

"NO!" I shouted, gasping for breath. My chest clenched and I felt a muscle spasm rip through my neck, cramping my throat.

He would stab him through the heart.

No!

I gasped for air. My vision was blotted with gray spots and I grew dizzy. The ropes around my wrists were tight, so tight. There was no blood. I couldn't escape. I would die here in a bed of my own piss.

"Help!" I called, my voice rasping between shallow breaths. There was no air in the room. I was choking, choking. There was no air at all, no matter how much I gasped. The room spun around me.

He would kill him. Kill him. *Kill.*

"Gav..." I cried weakly, and then everything went black.

Gav

I did something stupid.

Before, I'd said that I was not a stupid person - I always made my moves carefully, cautiously, rationally. If I slipped up, I might get caught, and I knew what the consequences were if anyone discovered me.

But I was curious. Like my kitten.

And so I did a stupid, careless thing. I went back to the library where I had seen the girl. I told myself I was going to pick up some more books for her to read, to keep her company. But that was only another lie that I told myself.

The truth of it was, I wanted to know more about her.

As I walked in, I darted a quick cross-glance over to the counter. Her friend was nowhere to be seen, and whether that was good news or bad news I couldn't decide. I made my way over to the elevator and got inside.

This was where she had kissed me. The impertinent girl. Thinking about it now made me heat up - her soft body against my chest, her hungry lips seizing mine. I licked my lips and pressed the button to go up.

On the third floor, the elevator jerked to a stop. Wandering aimlessly down the aisles, I let my fingers run across the spines of the books. Crime novels, science fiction tomes. Romance novels down at the corner, their spines red and gold and well-worn.

Fiction. This was all a fiction, I thought. My kitten, back at home, tied safely to the bed - all of it was a story that I told myself. A story that led, in every possible path, towards a tragic ending.

Tragic, for how else could this story end? It was impossible that we would figure out a way to live together. Outside of the house, she had seemed so happy, so enchanted with the world. And for all my pretensions at objectivity, she had managed to slip underneath, into my calm world, and ripple the surface with her desires.

At the end of the row of books, I turned around, then stopped dead in my tracks.

It was her friend, the other girl. She was sitting

down in the middle of the aisle, a handful of books at her side. Her hair was dyed green where before it had been purple, and there were dark circles under her eyes, but it was her.

This was why I had come here, but now that the girl was in front of me I didn't know how to react. Recognition flashed over her face as she looked up at me, but if I hadn't been looking for it, I wouldn't have found it.

"Can I help you?"

Her voice sounded tired, and although her words were polite, she narrowed her eyes while looking at me. Not blinking.

"Just browsing. I've seen you here before, haven't I?"

She rolled her eyes and thumbed toward her face. I didn't know whether she was pointing at the piercings or the hair, or both.

"Can't miss me," she said.

"You worked with that girl, didn't you? The one who ran away?"

"She didn't run away."

Now her face sharpened into rapt attention. I could almost smell her suspicion. Rather than make me cautious, though, her suspicion emboldened me. Here I was, right where I had met her. It almost made me understand those killers who leave notes or other clues. Before I thought that they were trying to get caught, but right now, standing next to the one girl who could link us together, the world was so bright that I couldn't even remember the shadow.

"I'm sorry," I said. "I saw on TV—"

"That's what they're all saying," she said. She ran a hand through her hair, brushing her green bangs back. Under all the eyeliner and metal, she was actually quite a beautiful girl. Not my type, but classically pretty. "Even her parents."

"You don't believe them?"

"I don't—look, I'm sorry. I don't know what to believe. Kat wasn't that kind of girl."

"You knew her well?"

"Well enough." She squinted up at me. "How did you know her?"

"I don't. I only met her here that one day. When she was working with you." My voice was calm, smooth, remembering all the details. The romance novel on the cart.

"I can see how you would remember *me*," she said, tossing her green bangs back. "But how did you remember *her*?"

"Well, she did kiss me."

Now the girl's eyes widened.

"She *what*?"

My mind stumbled. Kat had told me that it had been a bet. That this girl had bet her to kiss me. Was that a lie?

"She kissed you? Are you *serious*?" The girl stood up,

"I—I mean, yes, she kissed me. Out of nowhere. I didn't know her before, and when she asked me on a date I said I wasn't interested. I was dating someone else at the time, you see."

I clamped my mouth shut, stopping myself before I rambled off into a world of explanatory lies. Only liars ever gave explanations without being asked.

"Wow."

The girl leaned on the wall of books, and a title caught my eye: *Caught In the Act*. I blinked my eyes back to her face.

"So she really did kiss you. I didn't think she had the balls to do it."

I shrugged, affecting nonchalance.

"When I saw her on TV, I thought: *what a coincidence*. One day she's flirting with me, the next day…" I waved my hand away into the air.

"She told me that she chickened out," the girl said in a half-whisper.

"I'm sure she didn't want to bother me after I'd turned her down. You really think she didn't run away? You think something else happened to her?" I leaned forward, and the girl looked up at me, frightened.

"I don't know." The girl shook her head, her bangs and earrings swinging in the air. "I mean, she had her demons, we all do. God, I don't know anymore. She told me that she would never do something like that again, but… I don't know. Maybe she was lying about that, too."

"What was she like?" I asked softly.

"Kat? She was great. Funny, smart. She would have been finished with school already, except for all the loan stuff. I told her—"

Her eyes welled up suddenly with tears. Trembling, her lips pressed together so tightly they went white.

"I told her she was boring," she said. "I called her a slacker. That was the last thing I said to her."

Her face contorted with grief. I had the thought of

putting a comforting hand on her shoulder, but that would be worse than nothing. The cause of her grief was standing right in front of her, and there was no way for me to fix it.

"Excuse me," she said. Her hand wiped away tears, held back her sniffling. "I—I have to go now."

"I'm sorry about your friend," I said. "I hope they find her."

She nodded and fled, leaving the books on a pile in the middle of the aisle next to the cart. I could hear her sobbing as she walked down the aisle, her feet nearly running away from me.

CHAPTER TWENTY-TWO

Gav

When I got back home, the house was quiet.

"Kat?"

I called her name as I walked up the bedroom stairs, holding the books I'd picked out for her. Hopefully these were better. A couple of suspense novels, and a book of short stories. A bit more literary than the romances I'd originally picked out.

"Sorry I took so long. I—"

I stopped in the doorway. My heart stopped too.

Kat's head lolled to one side, grotesquely. Her eyes were closed.

The books dropped to the floor as I strode forward. The smell of urine hit me as I leaned over the bed.

"Kat? Kat!"

I shook her shoulder, but she didn't move. Quickly I pressed my ear to her chest. My heart was pounding so hard that I could barely hear over it, but it was there. Her heartbeat. She wasn't dead.

Stupid. Stupid, to leave her chained up with no way to get to the bathroom. I needed locks on the outside of the bedroom door. I needed—

I needed her to wake up.

Shaking, I untied the knots that bound her wrists. Her hands were limp and white, cool in the air. I rubbed her wrists with my thumbs, urging the circulation back into them.

"Kat? You're okay, Kat. You're okay." I whispered the words like a chant, like a prayer. Had she fainted? I went into the bathroom and turned on the cold faucet in the bath. I took a washcloth and ran it under the stream of water. And ammonia—I could use ammonia.

I fumbled through the cabinet, trying to find the inhalant. It would be a last resort. There it was. I tucked the bottle into my pocket.

I ran back out to the bed and pressed the washcloth to her forehead. Her lips fell apart but there was no other sign of motion, just her breath, warm against my arm. The water dripped down her cheeks like tears. It turned her hair dark brown with moisture.

"Kat! Kat!" I shouted desperately, choking on her name. Still she would not open her eyes.

This—this was my guilt, my true sin. All of my life, I'd known that I was different. I did not care for others. I had a horrible urge to kill, to destroy. And now, through my own stupidity, I'd destroyed the one thing I'd come to care for.

"Please wake up, kitten. Please."

My hands flitted over her body, squeezing her limbs as though that would bring her back from wherever she was. And in the back of my head, the shadow taunted me.

This is what you wanted.

"No," I said. "Kat, wake up."

This is the easiest way. Cut her up. Burn her. Like the others—

"No!" I howled the word so loudly that she must

wake up, she must. The thought of taking a knife to her body made me as ill as I had been when I'd tried to cut my own wrist, and it was with great effort that I suppressed the bile threatening to rise in my throat. But she slept on, unhearing.

The only noise in the room was the sound of water running from the bathroom.

"Come on," I said. I flung away the red ropes from her wrists. Carefully, I gathered her up into my arms, not caring about the wetness soaking her lower half.

The bath was shallow, a few inches of water. The rush of the cold water filled my ears. I had no hope. In my arms, I thought I already carried a dead woman.

I knelt.

"Please," I whispered, not knowing who I whispered to. Supporting her neck with my arm, I lowered her into the cold bath. I picked up the ammonia inhalant, pressed it under her nose.

Her body convulsed. Her back arched against the ceramic bathtub - I caught her head before it hit the hard tile. And then—*oh, God, and then*—my kitten opened her eyes.

She gasped once, a breath of air sucked hard into her lungs. Her hands flailed, clutching at my chest and splashing water over the side of the tub. Her eyes were wide with fear, and as she inhaled gulps of air I supported her back, gave her room to breathe. Relief washed over me, driving away the shadow with the fear of her death.

"Gav—" she said, her throat hoarse. Her breaths came in shudders through her body.

I clasped her hands, pulled her to me, held her tight.

"It's alright," I said. "Don't be afraid. I'm here. It's alright."

Kat

The water in the bath was so cold that when I woke up I thought I was drowning in an icy lake. Gav held me against his chest and I sucked in deep breaths, trying to comfort myself. Trying not to panic. The world refocused in my vision.

Finally I got control of my breathing, and I sat up with Gav's help in the bath. Goosebumps ran down my arms and legs, and I shivered, reaching forward to turn off the cold water. Gav saw what I was reaching for and turned on the hot water instead. I lay back and took deep breaths as the water in the tub warmed up.

"What happened?" I asked, looking up.

"I might ask the same of you," he said.

I shook my head. My hands and feet felt numb, but with the new warm water they were beginning to tingle with feeling.

"I… I passed out. I was having a panic attack. I—"

Immediately the reason for my panic attack struck me again. Fear closed around my throat, clenching shut my windpipe.

"Did you kill him?" I asked.

"Who?"

Gav stared at me dumbly. I grabbed his arm, my fingers digging into his skin.

"The man. Did you kill him?"

"No. Kat, are you alright? I'm so sorry I left you for so long. I didn't even think—I thought I'd be back before you woke up—"

"You didn't kidnap him? That wasn't why you left last night?"

Gav shook his head. I breathed out, my shoulders relaxing.

"I went to the library to get more books," he said. "And when I came back, I saw you there…"

He looked so different. I couldn't put my finger on what it was until he spoke again.

"I thought you were dead," he said. And then I realized what it was.

It was emotion.

I reached out my hand and touched his cheek. How strange, that emotion can change a person's face so much. His eyes looked softer around the edges, deeper somehow. Then I drew my hand back. He had gotten me drunk, tied me up. Left me tied up in bed while he went out. No matter how much relief I felt, it wasn't enough to forgive him for everything he had done. For all the things he had done.

"Let me clean up," I said, realizing that I'd pissed all over myself before passing out. The smell came through my nostrils and I was shocked to realize I hadn't even noticed it before. "The bed—"

"I'll get it. Don't worry. Are you sure you're okay?"

"I'm fine. It was just a panic attack. I hyperventilated. I'll be okay."

"Don't lock the bathroom door, alright? I want to

make sure you're not going to pass out again."

A bubble of laughter rose up in my throat. A serial killer, a maniac, a man who had kidnapped me and tied me up in his basement—he was telling me not to lock the door behind me? It was so ridiculous I could scream. Instead I nodded and pulled my knees up to my chest.

I let the bathtub drain as I pulled the dress off of me. The fabric was wet and heavy, clinging to my skin, but there was no way I was asking Gavriel to come back in and help me out of it. He'd done enough already.

The hot water I splashed over myself felt so good that I lingered while soaping myself, cross-legged in the bottom of the tub. Gav called into the bathroom once, and I answered him, but other than that he left me alone.

I wrapped a towel and came out to see him sitting on the bed. The sheets had been changed out, and there was a new bedspread across the mattress, this one a light green. He looked up at me as though I was a ghost. I sat down on the bed, my heart thumping. I didn't know whether I was more relieved or angry.

"I thought you were dead," he repeated.

"I thought you were going to kill someone else."

"I wasn't."

"And I wasn't dead. Even if I was, what does it matter?"

"Kat—"

My name sounded so strange coming out of his mouth. Especially now that he looked at me with such tenderness.

"We had a deal. A trade."

"Only for one day—"

"It scared me so much," I said, interrupting him. I

couldn't stop now. We had to talk about this, or else every time he left I would be met with the same terror, the same panic attack. "When you left, I couldn't even breathe. Unless you can get me more pills—"

"I can't."

"Then you can't go out like that. You can't kill anyone else. We had a trade, remember? We should be able to trade again."

"It was a fair trade. Being with you… it helps drive the urge away. It's not quite the same, the thrill of it, but… but it's close. It helps."

"You said there were other girls."

"Not anymore," he said. "I can't exactly bring women home anymore. Not with you here."

"No, but couldn't you, you know? Go back to their place instead?"

Even as I spoke the words, a thick band of jealousy wrapped around my heart. I tried to let it go. I hated Gav, at least that's what I told myself. But even sitting here, I could feel his desire radiating out toward me. I could feel my own attraction, too, entwined with his.

He shook his head, as though dismissing a long-considered possibility.

"It's not the same. With them, it's only a sexual release. With you, there's—I can't explain. There's a brightness to it."

He touched my hand, his fingers slipping under my palm.

"Maybe it's the idea that you're mine. Forever. That I can do what I want with you. That I can kill you, if I want. Even if I wouldn't. I *wouldn't*." He spoke the last words quickly, squeezing my hand in his. "Whatever it is, it makes it go away. The urge."

I shivered. This, *this* was what I wanted? It couldn't be. And yet I did not draw my hand away from his.

"I talked with your friend. She misses you."

I was so shocked that I almost dropped the towel. I clenched the terrycloth to my chest.

"She said you were a great person. Really smart. She wished she had told you that before you left."

"Does she think I ran away?"

"No."

I nodded sadly. Jules was the one person I knew would take up for me. She knew why I had run away before. As I thought about her, my eyes burned with tears. I would never see her again, not as long as I was stuck here.

Gav sat, watching me, his hand warm under mine.

"Why are you telling me this?" I asked. He dropped his gaze to my fingers. His thumb, muscled and thick, rolled around my small fingers, squeezing them.

"I don't know. I'm glad you're not dead."

"I can't stay here."

"You can't leave."

It was not the truth I wanted to hear. Damn him! To never talk to anyone else - to never see Jules, to never walk in freedom outside. To be leashed, constantly, always on the end of a line connected to him.

I pulled my hand away. It was the only thing I could do. My one act of resistance, however small. He stood up from the bed.

"I'll put a lock on the outside of the bedroom door, so I can leave you inside here when I go out. I'll do it this evening."

He made to go, and I realized that there was one more thing I could do.

"Gav?"

"Yes?"

"Don't leave again. Don't kill him."

It was a sacrifice. A *trade*. But then again, what was I sacrificing? My life was nothing here. It meant nothing. Until I died or escaped, I would be nothing. And until then, I could keep him from killing. That was the only place I could make meaning.

This is what I told myself. I rejected any attraction I had toward him, repudiated it. If I was to let him touch me, it would be for this reason only.

And yet, secretly, I knew that it was not the reason at all.

"Kat?"

He spoke my name. He had no right to speak my name like that, the sound tripping off of his tongue in a way that made my insides clench with desire. Desire and hate.

"Stay with me," I said.

"Why?" he asked.

"Because I don't want you to kill again."

"You're a liar, kitten," he said gently. "You lie to me. You lie to yourself."

"Stay with me," I said desperately. "A trade. Do whatever you want to me."

He smiled. And the way he smiled made me feel as though I was already on the kitchen table, waiting for him to stab me through the heart.

CHAPTER TWENTY-THREE

Gav

When I installed the locks on the door, she did not even look at me. Her nose was buried in her book, a thriller. Her eyes stayed glued in one place, though, and she did not turn the page once. I could sense her eyes tracking me in her peripheral vision.

An interesting fact - when you see something in the corner of your eye, everything is black and white. The light entering at such an extreme angle doesn't hit the central cones and rods that show color. I wondered what shade of gray she saw in me. I turned to her and saw her eyes flit down the page.

"Tonight, what do you want me to do?" I asked.

"Nothing."

"You said—"

"You can do anything you want to do to me. That's the trade."

Irritation scraped at my nerves.

"I'm giving you a chance to make it easier on yourself, kitten."

"I don't want it to be easier."

"You like it rough?" I stood at the foot of the bed. "No, don't answer. I'll just do whatever I think you'll like."

She didn't say a word.

I came over next to her on the bed and lay beside her. As I slid my hand over her chest, her breath caught in her throat. I measured her heartbeat. It was slow, steady.

I nuzzled my face into her hair and pressed my mouth against her neck. Her heart jumped under my hand.

"How do you like the book?"

She whimpered.

I licked the soft spot at the end of her jawline, sucked softly at the skin there. Then harder.

"Oh!"

"Not the best writing? You haven't turned the page since I've been here."

She shut the book with more force than was necessary and let it fall to her side.

Her scent was enough to make me hard, and I pressed against her. As she stared silently at the ceiling, her tongue came out to moisten her bottom lip.

"Tell me you don't want me," I said, teasing.

"No."

"Then tell me you want me."

"No."

This time her voice was a whisper. A lie.

Her heart raced under my palm. Slowly, carefully, I eased myself away from her. This was dangerous, and I could not take her now. Not now. I struggled to keep myself from pinning her down, taking her right then.

If she could not make up her mind, I would not make it for her. For the first time in a long time, I found myself wanting something I could not have, and although I wanted to take it, I could not bring myself to.

I turned at the doorway and looked at her out of the corner of my eye. Dim gray curves in my bed.

The new brass lock on the door shone brightly in front of me. I touched the deadbolt with my finger. Cool metal. I wanted to touch her, her warm skin, her deliciously tender breasts.

"Don't kill anyone while you're out there."

"I won't," I said. She was teasing, yet not teasing. I struggled to find the words to ask what I wanted to ask.

"When I come back…" I trailed off. I had never felt so uncertain, so uncomfortable around anyone. I felt as though I had opened up a part of myself that I should not have opened. It irritated me, grated on my nerves. Did she really care about me? And why did it matter?

"Do what you want," she said.

What more could I ask for?

The bar I went to had a crowd of people on one end, near the pool tables. For a moment I considered leaving, but then I thought of Kat and sat down at the other end of the bar, next to a middle-aged biker.

This would be her first test with the lock. Would she try to escape? I had waited a while downstairs before leaving and heard nothing coming from the room. But she was smarter than I had given her credit for before.

I would not make that mistake again. One drink, maybe two, and then I would return.

The uncertainty that had grabbed hold of me was astounding. In my own home, I felt like an intruder. Watching her on the bed, I felt out of my element. Uneasy.

I'd never felt uneasy before.

I gulped down the whiskey I'd ordered. The liquid

burned as it slid down the back of my throat, easing the irritation. What was it about her that had gotten so far under my skin?

"Hard day?" the bartender asked.

"Why?" I snapped my head up.

"You just look a bit out of it," he said. "Another one?"

I looked down to see an empty glass in front of me. With a single finger, I pushed it forward. He tilted the bottle of whiskey and flooded the glass again.

Out of it. Out of my mind? Out of character, that was for sure. Mentally I ticked off the alarming symptoms. Guilt, something that had never afflicted me before. Irritation and unease. Worry.

"I should kill her," I muttered.

"Mine, too," the man sitting next to me said.

"Excuse me?"

"My wife. You can kill 'er too." His words were slurred, drunken.

At the other end of the bar the group of people cheered a good pool shot. A woman leaned over the pool table, her breasts hanging like pendulums. Her chest was wrinkled, the epidermis stretched and spotted from years of tanning.

"Oh," I said.

"Damn bitches. If it ain't one thing, it's another. Nag, nag, nag. You can't do anything right with 'em. Don't even bother trying, am I right?"

He held his beer bottle up and clinked it hard against my glass. My empty glass. I raised a finger and ordered another. The bartender obliged.

"She kick you out of the house?" the man said, his

smiling face disgustingly ruddy.

"No," I said.

The bar was growing dark, or maybe it was just me. Or the shadow. I blinked and looked around. It had come back, yes. She had distracted me from it, but she was not here now. I felt the numbness of the shadow creep into the edges of my mind.

"Outta my way, Sharon!" One of the drunken men elbowed the woman next to the pool table. Tattoos sleeved both of his thick arms, peeking out from under his stained white tee.

"You can't get that shot," she snapped back, moving unhappily back, arms crossed.

"Jus' gotta get away sometime, I hear you," the ruddy man next to me said. I breathed in, trying to find air.

"You feelin' okay?" His beer breath assaulted me. I pushed back my stool from the bar. Everything was dark. I could barely see the edge of the bar in front of me.

"I… I just need to think."

Glass shattered on the floor next to the pool table. I closed my eyes.

"You dumb fucking bitch!"

A slap. A scream.

Then the bar was gone, and in front of me was the tattooed man, his face snarling. I snapped my fist across his face. The sound of bone snapping. Waves of shadow darkened my vision, made it impossible for me to see anything except in flashes.

My fists. Blood. More blood. Pouring from his nose, his split lip.

Pain, total blackness. My ears ringing.

We were on the ground, me on top of him. The woman was screaming behind me, pulling at my shirt.

"Get off of him! Get off of him!"

The shadow laughing, laughing at me as I swung my fists down over and over again. I did not care about the pain in my knuckles. Gone were the guilt, the uncertainty, the irritation. In their place came pure satisfaction.

Bones shattered. The zygomatic bone under the eyes. The infraorbital—oh, god, it felt good. The crack, the shudder, the bursting blood vessels. Blood everywhere, washing the shadow away. Then somebody pulled me off of him, and before I could fight back I was outside of the bar, panting hard, blood running down my knuckles.

Feeling supremely unfulfilled.

Kat

I tried the door as soon as he left. I had replaced doors before, but he had sealed the pins holding the hinges in place.

In the closet, I scrounged for anything that could help. A hammer, a screwdriver, anything. The shelf at the top of the closet was too high for me to reach. I grabbed the armchair from the side of the bed and dragged it over. On tiptoe, my fingers searched the shelf and hit something hard.

A toolbox? My body tensed as I found a grip on the edge of the box.

I pulled the wood box out and immediately knew it wasn't what I was looking for. A cherry colored wood, smooth and polished to a shine.

Curious, I sat down in the chair with the box on my lap. Inside, there were a few pairs of earrings, necklaces, rings. And a photo. I picked up the photo and turned it over.

A young boy with dark hair and light eyes, holding the hand of a woman who looked just like him.

My face turned hot and I dropped the photo as quickly as if it had turned to fire. It fluttered back down into the jewelry box. A mistake. I shouldn't have looked inside here. A sickness gripped my heart.

Although I had been locked up in here for days, now was the first time that I felt I had to escape. The room had turned warm, the air stifling.

Slam!

I jerked my head up. The door had crashed open and Gavriel was standing in the entryway. The jewelry box clattered to the floor as I started up to my feet, and the photo tumbled down after the heavier things. He stared, eyes wide.

His hair was damp with sweat. Blood dripped down his arms to the tips of his fingers. As I watched, a drop of blood fell to the floor. He had cuts along his knuckles, and his skin had taken on a pallor that made him look almost like a vampire. But his eyes were the scariest.

His eyes looked at me completely blankly, as though I was just a ghost. The same way he had looked at me before, when we'd first met. Like he was dead, or I was.

"What happened?" I asked. The question sounded ridiculous to me in the open air.

"I didn't kill anyone," he said. He walked over and sat on the edge of the bed, looking down at his hands. He flexed his fists, the cuts bleeding freely.

"What... what—"

"You were looking through my things."

He stared up at me from the bed. He wasn't accusing me. He wasn't guilting me. He was simply stating a fact. It disarmed me completely. I fell to my knees and began to scoop up the jewelry. When I got to the photo, he was already there in front of me. His hand reached down and took it before I could.

Kneeling in front of me. Staring, that awful, beautiful stare. He captivated me. His fingers stained the picture with blood as his thumb moved along the edge.

Did you do it? I wanted to ask. I wondered how dark he truly was. I wondered if he was really a monster. But I couldn't. And then, as though reading my mind, he responded.

"My father killed her."

If I hadn't already been sitting on the floor, I would have fallen to my knees in surprise. His eyes shone with tears, and when he blinked they streamed from the corners of his eyes down his cheeks.

"He was like me," Gav continued. "He lived with a shadow over him. He was full of darkness."

The words were wrenched from his throat, and he choked on the last, a sob stopping his throat. He bent his head.

"Go to the closet."

His voice was flat. It would not tolerate disobedience. Shakily, I got to my feet and turned to the closet.

"There's a smaller cardboard box near the one you found. Have you looked inside it yet?"

I shook my head. I didn't trust my voice to speak.

"Reach up and find it."

I stood up on the chair. The hot flush under my skin felt like burning now.

"Do you have it?"

I touched cardboard, pulled it out.

"Yes," I said. I sat down on the chair, too scared to look at him. He had hurt somebody tonight. Would he hurt me?

"Open it."

"What's—"

"Open it."

The worst sentence I've ever heard. The amount of pain in his voice was staggering. He wasn't faking this; I was sure of it. But I didn't know what to expect when I opened the box. It was more photos. But these were not happy photos, not like the one in the jewelry box. These were all Polaroids, so dark that for a moment I didn't understand what I was seeing. Then I did.

My stomach heaved. The top Polaroid was the same little boy. This time he was wearing only underwear. His body—

Oh, God. Oh dear God.

The boy was naked. His body was covered in bruises.

"Look at them," he ordered. I froze, my hands clenching the cardboard box so tightly my fingernails dug back into my cuticles.

"Please—"

"Look."

I couldn't say no to him. I picked up the photographs with trembling hands and went through them. The second photograph made me lean forward and retch dry air.

He was bound with rope, his underwear dirty. His back was discolored: yellow and purple streaks and the edged impression of a belt, over and over again marked into his skin. Tears burned my eyes.

"Look," he said again, his voice duller. I looked. It was too much. I couldn't look away, and the only thing that saved me was the blurring of my tears. The photographs showed the life of a tortured child, instant by agonizing instant. The record of a body so damaged by bruises that they had worked their way to the inside.

"Who could do such a thing?" I whispered.

"This is what I look at before I go out to kill them," he said. "This is all I see when I tie them down, when I slice them open. I see all this darkness. It overwhelms me. It creeps into my vision. There's only one way I can get rid of it: I cut it out."

He left me there, in the room, crying over the photos of a boy who had lost his innocence a long time ago. He washed his hands and brushed his teeth and crawled into bed.

My sobs subsided. My gasps for air turned to shuddering breaths, and then to a slow inhale, exhale. I put the boxes away and turned off the light.

Then I crawled in next to him and held him tightly. His arm curled around me. Without speaking, he folded me against his chest and we lay there, bodies tangled, cradling each other until we fell asleep.

It was then that I realized I was the one torturing him.

CHAPTER TWENTY-FOUR

Kat

I woke before him in the morning. His arm was curled over my shoulder, and his lips grazed my forehead. When I shifted, he murmured, his lips moving against my skin like butterfly wings.

When I was a kid, I caught a butterfly in a glass jar. I remember taking it out and holding it in my hands. My mother scolded me.

"Its wings are delicate," she said. "Just brushing them with your fingertips will destroy them. It'll never be able to fly again."

I felt the same way now. Without knowing, I had touched something delicate, something horribly damaged. I didn't know what to do to keep from damaging him any more.

I did not want him to leave, but I did not know if I could force him to stay.

"Kitten," he murmured.

"I'm here," I said softly. The morning light had turned the room gray, but when he opened his eyes I saw the glint of blue-green that always swirled there below the surface.

"You didn't leave."

"Your arm was kind of in the way."

He smiled and rolled over. I felt cold without the

touch of his skin on me as he sat up on the edge of the bed.

Had we really slept together like this? Like lovers, entwined like two strands of frayed rope amid the silken sheets?

Was I falling for this monster? Was he a monster?

My eyes refocused on his back and I saw that he was looking at me. I reached out and touched his skin gently. Imagining the belt. Imagining the bruises.

Don't touch the butterfly's wings.

"What do you want from me?" he asked.

"What?"

"Today. Do you want the same thing?"

I wanted to tell him the truth: that all I wanted... was him. I wanted him to stay with me, to hold me, to pin me down and torture me with kisses like he had the first time. God, I wanted all this and so much more. But I couldn't let him know how much of a hold he really had over me.

Not for the first time, I wondered if this was all a trick. Then I remembered the photos of the boy, and I swallowed my doubt. No, he was real. This was all real. The note of desire that crept into his speech when he talked to me, that was real too.

"What do you want?" he repeated, wearily. As though preparing himself for the Sisyphean task ahead: to try not to kill anyone today.

"I don't know." I didn't say the things I wanted to say. *Come to bed. Kiss me.*

Make me yours.

"How about a trade?"

He sounded so reasonable. So rational. As though I

was a fair partner in this deal. He knew it wasn't true. But I finally understood a corner of that sorrow that had been beaten into him. I understood the need for him to pull a veil over what he was doing.

He was not the only one here who was ashamed of the past.

"A trade."

"Question for question."

"That means you're staying."

"That's part of the trade. But that also means you're staying with me."

The hint of desire in the curve of his lip. I saw all of the little things. I saw them, but did he want me to see them? Was he twisting me around him again with emotion?

I couldn't shove the thought back into a dark corner of my brain. It was apparent in every movement he made.

He wanted me.

And I wanted him.

It may be delusion, but if it was, then it was the most delicious delusion I had ever tasted. His touch sent shivers of sparks through me that danger alone could not account for.

I wanted the soft part of him, yes, the lover, the charmer. The gentleman. But I also wanted the part of him that was raw and rough, the part of him that tied me up. The side that dressed perfectly because perfection was expected.

I could not be perfect, I thought, looking down at my wrists. Of all the imperfections of my body, these were the ones that would stay forever.

"Question for question."

"So that you can know more about me. And I can know more about you."

"Who goes first?"

He smiled.

"I knew you would want to play," he said.

"How did you know?"

"Because you're a curious little kitten, that's why," he said, falling back onto his side next to me. His hand caressed my cheek, holding me in the palm of his hand. Possessive.

"Okay," I said. "You go first."

His hand stroked the underside of my chin idly.

"What's the first thing you remember?"

"The very first thing?"

"And no bullshit about remembering when you left the womb. Those aren't real memories."

"No. I remember..."

I closed my eyes and thought back. Back to when I was four, maybe five.

"I remember my mom taking me on a picnic in the park. There was a field, a huge field of clover. It probably wasn't that big, not really, but to me it looked like an ocean of green. My mom told me to look for a four-leaf clover. If I found one, it would be lucky."

"Did you find one?"

I shook my head.

"I didn't even look. There was a dandelion, big and yellow, and I picked that instead. You remember what they said when we were kids? You had to smell the dandelion while thinking about someone you love. And if your nose turned yellow that meant they loved you back."

"Who did you think about?"

"I didn't think about anyone. Is that weird? I didn't care about that. I wished for my parents to love each other instead."

"And?"

"It didn't work. I don't even remember getting home from the picnic. I must have blocked it out. He… I don't think he loved anyone. I don't know why my mom stayed with him."

"It's hard to leave. My mother didn't leave, either."

His hand had stopped moving against my skin. I could tell that he was off in the past, thinking about it.

"You couldn't have done anything to stop it."

His eyes narrowed, found mine.

"How do you know that?"

"You can't do anything when it's like that. They're not going to change. I thought—I thought that if I stopped asking for toys, stopped wanting anything, that my dad would be happier. I thought that if I stayed locked inside myself that he wouldn't be bothered by me. I didn't want to be a burden at all. I didn't want to make him angry. But it didn't work."

"It wasn't you."

"Tell that to a five-year old kid," I said, laughing sadly. "But it wasn't you, either. You couldn't have stopped him."

"I could have killed him," he said.

I was quiet. There wasn't any anger in his eyes, only regret.

"Where's your father now?" I asked.

"I don't know," he said. "If I knew, I would have

killed him already. Sometimes I think that's the only way to stop the shadow from coming back. But I've looked and looked. He got away."

"I'm sorry."

"I've stopped looking for him. Maybe he's dead already."

The silence between us was so intimate. I wanted to lean forward and kiss him, hug him, pull him into my arms and tell him that it would be alright. But there was nothing that would be alright, not with him. Not with me.

"Your turn," I whispered.

"What can I do now?" he asked. He didn't expect an answer - it sounded more like a cry to heaven than a real question.

How could I answer him? I didn't know what it was like to be a killer. I didn't know what it was like to want to murder people, to have that dark of a need. I reached up and took his hand, brought it to my lips. All the while I looked into his eyes.

If I was never going to escape this place, I could do this for him.

"I want you to take it out on me," I said. "Everything."

His desperation turned into something else. His eyes boiled with emotion, so strange after seeing him blank for so long. The room was growing brighter with the rising sun.

"I don't want to kill you," he said, his voice cracking.

"Don't kill me. Come close. Hurt me. Here."

I lifted my wrists to him. What was I asking him?

For exactly what you want.

There was a part of me, long hidden, that had desires. Dark desires. When he'd bound me by my wrists and tortured me with his tongue, they had come out. When his hand spanked my skin red, they had screamed with pleasure. I wanted this. I wanted him. I wanted to be his.

"Tie me up," I said. "Do whatever you need to do. I want it too."

He looked up at me.

"You don't want it. Not really. If you knew what my shadow wanted—"

"You're not the only one with the shadow," I whispered.

He paused for a moment, his eyes searching mine.

"I wanted to die for so long," I said, my voice hoarse with emotion. "I didn't feel anything but a numb kind of pain. When I'm with you... it goes away."

"I'll hurt you." He said it so softly the words felt invisible.

"I want you to hurt me."

"Badly. I might leave marks."

I turned my wrists around, showing off the only scars I had.

"I'm already marked. Besides," I said, "who else is going to see them?"

Gav

Take it out on me, she said. And here the shadow slipped, revealing an emotion I haven't felt in a while.

Fear.

Her wrists defied me to hurt her. How could I hurt her more than she had already been hurt?

"Why would you do this?" I asked.

"I'm trapped here."

She stopped trying to beg me. Stopped trying to plead. Instead, she spoke calmly and rationally. Prescribing a course of action for my disease.

"Is there any other alternative?" she asked. "If you don't want to kill me…"

"I don't want to hurt you."

That was a lie. I wanted to turn her flesh red and make her scream. But I wanted to please her at the same time. I wanted to plunge myself into her. I wanted to shatter her and put her back together.

"You're too late. I can't be hurt anymore. Not by you. Not by anyone."

I took her wrists in my hand and pulled them up over her head. Her eyes went wide with fright. She was right to be frightened. I was frightened by what I was going to do.

"We'll see, kitten," I said.

Kat

I couldn't stop looking at him as he got out the

rope.

"Put out your hands," he said. I did. I was obedient, a good pet, playing along even though it wasn't a game anymore. The rest of my life was here with him, and I told myself I might as well enjoy it. But there was no need to pretend. When he wrapped the rope around my wrists four times, a thrill ran up my arms.

As he tightened the knot around the middle, I couldn't help but smile. I was scared. I was already thinking about what he would do to me once he had me all tied down. Before, I was ashamed, thinking about what people would say if they knew I went along willingly. But there was a lightness that I hadn't felt in a long, long while. Nobody was here to see me, nobody was ever going to know.

Nobody would know that I wanted this. No one except him.

The knots tied my wrists together this time, and he wrenched them above my head.

"Why are you smiling, kitten?"

His free hand slid down roughly over my body.

"Because I want this."

For the first time in a long time, I let myself feel desire. The ache between my legs grew as his hand slid down between my thighs, and I embraced the ache, let it grow.

He kissed me roughly, insistently, his lips tearing the breath away from my lungs. I gasped as he broke away from the kiss.

His cock was hard through his pants, against my leg. He breathed hot and fast, one hand still pinning my wrists above my head. His hand rumpled my dress up at my waist.

I could feel how much he wanted me, and it made me long for him to fill me. No longer did I feel ashamed. This was my body, my desire, and I owned it.

His hand was kneading my skin through the fabric. There was no way to take my dress off now that my wrists were bound together. I grinned.

"Should have undressed me before you tied me up," I said.

He slapped me across the face, hard. The shock of the blow ran through me like lightning, but he was kissing my lips before I could recover, biting my lower lip, sucking my flesh.

It hadn't been a slap to hurt, just to surprise. And it surprised me.

He swung a leg over my waist, straddled me. Before I could lower my arms he had grabbed the collar of my dress and ripped. The fabric tore easily in his fists. Soon my dress was nothing but scraps of silk over my naked body.

"You're not wearing underwear, kitten," he said. I lifted my chin.

God, I wanted him. His cock was hot and throbbing; I could feel it against my stomach as he leaned over. He kissed me so softly, so tenderly. The gentleness of his kiss sent me into a spiral of pure easy bliss, so easy that I began to drift away.

Then he twisted my nipple hard. Pain shot through my chest.

I yelped, bucking underneath him. He pinned my wrists back easily and licked the side of my neck, then bit down gently. The pain in my nipple had turned into a burning that ran hot through my nerves. I felt every bit of his touch as he grazed the top of my hot nipple with his thumb.

His fingers pinched down again, and I squealed. God, the heat! Despite the pain, I felt myself grow wet between my thighs.

"I'm going to suck you," he whispered. "Then I'm going to bite you."

I moaned as his mouth moved down below my ear, his tongue flicking my earlobe. He was careful not to let any part of him touch me between my thighs, where already I was aching.

His hand kneaded my shoulder muscle as his mouth took my nipple inside. His tongue slipped down, sliding along the underside of my breast. Then he sucked, and I inhaled sharply. It was a different kind of pain than before, and it seemed as though his lips were sucking me down where I desperately needed it. I twisted under his hold.

"Impatient kitten," he murmured.

"Please—"

His hand was at my throat, choking me. The pressure made me tight, my throat aching along with the rest of me. He kissed me on the lips as he choked me, stopping any attempts for breath.

"No," I tried to moan, but he pressed down harder, cutting off my air. I thrashed underneath him, my legs kicking. I didn't want this. I didn't want him to kill me! I wanted—

I wanted to live.

At the last second, he released my throat. I coughed, gasping for air. My throat wheezed as I tasted the delicious oxygen, drawing it deep into my lungs.

"Scared now, kitten?" he asked. His eyes blazed with desire, desire that I echoed. I wanted him, yes. I wanted him badly. I wanted everything he could offer. But I knew that he would only hurt me more if I told him this.

His fingers plunged between my thighs and I gasped. His lips parted and he brought his hand up, his skin gleaming with my moisture. He licked his fingers.

"You taste delicious."

I whimpered. I wanted his mouth on me, wanted him to ease the ache that shot through my core and made me twitch against the bedsheets.

"Do you want me to taste you, kitten?" he asked. There was a danger in his eyes.

"Yes," I said softly.

He smiled, a dangerous smile.

"It's too bad we're not doing what you want today."

Before I could even open my mouth to ask him what he meant, he had his hands on my hips. He flipped me over onto my stomach, and I landed hard, my breath rushing out of me. As I inhaled, he spanked me on the ass, his hand landing with a smack that sent a spasm through my body. I kicked out.

"Lift your ass up for me, kitten," he said.

I moaned, obeying. I raised myself to show him, in the most vulnerable position I had ever been in. Like a bitch in heat. It should have been degrading, but instead it turned me on intensely. I was so wet, I could feel my juices running down my thighs.

"Dirty kitten."

He spanked me again, then again. The fourth time,

my skin was so sensitive that it stung like flame. I jerked on the bed away from him, but he dragged me back. The spanks came hard and hot, sizzling on my skin. I cried out, twisting under his hands, but he did not stop. Every blow seared me, and despite the pain I began to rock back to meet him. I wanted it, every bit of pain, every fiery spank.

Then I felt his fingers slide down over my slit, stroking the outside part of me.

"Yes," I moaned. "Yes, please, oh god, please—"

He spanked me hard and I cried out.

"No begging, kitten," he said. "I'll do what I want to, when I want to, and nothing you say can stop it."

I choked out a sound of assent. His hand came back. Hot. Teasing. His fingers slid around the outside of my slick flesh, then probed in lightly.

More. Oh god, I needed more. I needed it now.

"Mmmmm," I said. I rocked back, trying to get him to put his fingers in farther. Again he spanked me. I cried out. This was agony, all of it, wanting him and hating him and needing him.

He thrust two fingers in up to his knuckle, and although it was not enough it was better than before. I bit down on the sheet in front of me and tried not to make any noise as he slid his fingers in and out. The rhythm was slow, his long hard fingers pressing, probing me.

Then I felt something else. His thumb, pressing at my asshole. I froze.

"Ah, kitten," he said. "Something that scares you?"

I breathed fast, trying not to move at all. I'd never done anything like this before, and it scared me, maybe more than anything else he'd done. His thumb circled the sensitive puckered flesh, making me clench. His two fingers continued their rhythm again, plunging deep into my slit. Sliding out. All the while his thumb circling, circling wet and slick around the place I'd never thought could feel good.

And it did feel good. His thumb massaged me, kneaded me, grazing over my opening and then pressing down on the muscled ring around it. When he finally pushed down with his thumb and entered me, though, I cried out, my body tensing around him. The aching pressure inside of me leapt to a new edge of desire. This was a sensation I'd never felt, and it sent thrills of pain and pleasure through me.

He left his thumb inside me, his fingers still working themselves in and out of my slick folds. I tightened and relaxed in alternating spasms, until my body relaxed around him, accepting him. Then he began to push again, his thumb penetrating me. He rolled the pad of his thumb around the inside of my pucker, slicking me with my own juices.

I groaned, feeling the pressure inside me build. There was something wrong with me that I liked this so much - the unfamiliar burn between my ass cheeks, the lightning sparking its way along my nerves as he thrust his fingers inside. I began to rock backwards, wanting more. I met his thrusting fingers, his probing thumb, and pushed him to go farther.

"Mmmmmm," I moaned, the noise buried in the sheets. His other hand spanked me, but it only made me rock back harder, wanting to feel the punishment with every nerve.

I was so close—so close to the edge. I could feel the

rumble of an orgasm beginning to find its purchase inside of me. I jerked my hips back, needing him to penetrate harder, deeper. Needing him—

Just then, he pulled away. I cried out in shock as my orgasm slipped away from me. My hips gyrated in the air, searching for the lost pressure, but searching in vain.

I twisted my neck to look back at him standing up at the edge of the bed. He wiped his hand on his pants, then unzipped.

His cock was huge, stiff and ready. I gasped, my mouth wet. All I wanted was for him to take me. I couldn't stand waiting another moment. He smiled.

"Tell me you want me, kitten. Tell me you want me to take you."

"I want you," I said, my voice shaky. "Gav, I want you so badly—"

Naked, he grabbed my legs, flipped me on my back. I squealed as he spread my thighs with his strong hands, then pinned my arms back like before. His cock slid over my swollen and slick folds, not penetrating, just hinting at what was to come.

"You destroy me," he whispered. His face looked so sincere that for a moment I wanted nothing more than for him to kiss me. He bent over me, the head of his cock probing at my entrance, then retreating. He reached for the bedside drawer and I heard the crinkle of a wrapper fall to the bed. I whimpered for him, lifting my hips in ready anticipation.

He filled me with one violent thrust. His eyes widened as he plunged into me, and I don't know what I looked like but I was screaming, screaming, already falling over the edge into an orgasm that shook my body to pieces.

He rocked back, then forward, rolling his hips deeper into my flesh. I felt my body stretch for him, clenching around him even as the climax shivered me. My legs wrapped around his waist, pulling him deeper.

I wanted him. I wanted him inside of me. I wanted every bit of him. He was a monster, yes, he was a villain, he was evil, and yet right then I needed him to take me, to own me. I wanted him to give me back my desires.

Sweat beaded on his lip as he plunged into me again and again, rolling his hips against mine. And I hadn't yet recovered from my first orgasm when I felt my body responding again with need, aching for another release that only he could give me.

The room was bright and now I could see clearly the blue and green and gray in his irises, gleaming brightly. His hand pinned down my hip as he thrust and I bucked against him, wanting him to control me. The ropes were tight around my wrists and I loved it, loved the feeling of giving myself over to every sensation that was happening at that very instant.

His rhythm grew faster, more insistent. I had thought that he had filled me entirely, but as he thrust he grew even stiffer, larger. His body rocked against mine, crashing body onto body in a whirlwind of slapping flesh, slick and ready.

"Ohhhh," I moaned, feeling myself grow ready for release. I twisted under him as he jackhammered between my thighs. His cock slammed into me again and again, harder and faster until I felt him jerk upwards, freezing at the apex of his thrust in a spasm.

I came at the same time, my body rippling with

pleasure as he jerked once, again, again, groaning in my ear. The sweet sound of his release. We clutched at each other needily, two dark souls in the middle of the strangest redemption.

He collapsed against me, his body almost crushing mine. I could feel his heartbeat racing against my own chest, our hearts trying to outdo each other. His lungs pressed against me with each breath.

And for the first time in a long time, I thought to myself:

I'm alive.

CHAPTER TWENTY-FIVE

___Gav___

The darkness receded as I spilled myself inside of her. The world brightened, the shadow gone.

For how long? I didn't care. What mattered was here, now.

What mattered was her.

She reached up to me and touched my lips. On her face was something like wonder.

"I love you," she said, and began to cry.

___Kat___

"I love you."

The words tumbled from my mouth and I lay there, more surprised that I had said them than surprised that I had felt them. Was it shock that drove me to tears? No, something else. A desperation that had grown inside of me until now, it showed itself.

He didn't say anything. Instead he stood up, stumbling at the edge of the bed.

"I'm sorry," he said.

I'm sorry? I wanted to reach out to him. Why are you sorry? Tears streamed down my cheeks and I was unable to stop them. I felt completely melted, unraveled. He had torn me apart inside and out, and I wanted him to turn to me, to hold me together. Instead he put his head in his hands.

"Please…" I whispered. "Gav?"

"Why are you crying?" he asked, a hint of frustration in his voice.

I shook my head. Strands of my hair stuck to my cheek, hot and wet as it was with tears.

"I don't know," I said. "It was wonderful. Gav—"

"And you're crying."

"This isn't real!" I sobbed.

There. That was it. That was the thing that made me cry right now. He had split open my heart, and I had given it away to an illusion.

The realization shattered me. All around me, the walls spun. He was there, sitting right there. He had touched me, made me feel alive. He had made me feel wanted. He had made me feel *loved*.

"This isn't real," I repeated. Trying to make myself believe what I knew to be the truth. "None of this is real."

"What isn't real?" His voice was blank, empty. It made me even angrier. I brought my fists down hard, but against the mattress they didn't even make a noise. My sobs were hoarse and angry.

"You!"

"I'm not real?"

He turned his head slowly, carefully meeting my gaze.

"You're a psychopath," I whispered. "The only guy who's ever cared about me is a psychopath."

"Does that make it not real?"

"But you don't care, not really. You don't care at all about me. I'm just a pet to you. I'm a prisoner. It's not real."

"You think you have it all figured out, kitten."

"I do."

"You're wrong." His voice lilted upward, as though teasing me. My throat burned.

"Tell me it's not true, then. Tell me you care about me."

"What would that serve?"

"It would help me be less lonely."

He turned, stood, his hands loose at both sides. He was naked, but standing over me I thought he looked for all the world like a warrior at the ready. The only thing missing was a knife in his hand.

"I care about you," he said.

"I don't believe you."

He spread his arms out, palms upward.

"What do you want?"

The air in the room was stale. My whole body rejected it. I curled up on my side, pulling the sheets over my shoulder. I had been so stupid. I had thought that when I reached out to him, he would reach back. But he wasn't human. He was a monster. And because I loved him, I was a monster, too.

"Nothing. I don't care."

"You don't care? Not even if I leave the house?"

I knew what he was saying. And yet my voice came out monotonous, uncaring. I didn't know if it was me who was speaking, or someone else.

"If you need to kill someone," I said, "kill me."

Gav

I wanted to vomit. I had defiled her, poor girl. I had poisoned her with myself, poisoned her with darkness.

And now she wanted to die.

I pulled my pants back on. Then I took the knife from my drawer. Her eyes didn't widen, but her pupils dilated as she looked at the blade in my hand.

Did she still think that I could kill her?

"I'm sorry," I said again. And yes, I was sorry. Guilt wracked me inside, made me sick with dread. She lay there still and naked, tear-streaked. Dirty with my sins. I went to the door.

"No," she said. "Gavriel."

"I'm sorry." The door closed behind me. And the padlock went on the bedroom door.

"No!" she yelled from behind the door. The lock snapped shut with a thick iron clank. Her steps to the door. Her fist pounding.

"No! Gav! _No!_"

"I'm sorry." This I said to myself as I walked down the stairs, down again to the basement, down, down.

It was dark on the floor of the basement where I lay down and closed my eyes. The shadow would always be a part of me. I wrapped myself up in shadows and I would not touch anything again. I wouldn't mar the outside world. Hours passed, hours and hours, and I did not eat, did not drink. I did not deserve release. I'd lied to myself about what I did. The men I killed were monsters, but I was worse than any of them.

I did not deserve anything but darkness.

CHAPTER TWENTY-SIX

Kat

When he took the knife out of the drawer, I froze.

Would he give me what I had asked for? I had told him to kill me, but as I spoke, watching him, I realized that I didn't want to die. He had made me feel alive, more alive than I had felt since I was young. And I wanted to live.

I almost smiled, weird as it was. Only after being threatened with murder, only after everything he had done to me... only now did I want to live.

But he didn't kill me. He didn't threaten me with the knife. Instead, he tucked it into his belt and left. I scrambled for the door as soon as I realized what he was doing.

"No! Gav!"

He was going to kill someone, I was sure of it.

I pounded on the doorframe, screaming at the top of my lungs.

"No! Don't do it!"

He heard me, I was sure of it. His footsteps walked away from the door, down the hallway. I pressed my ear to the door and heard him start to go down the stairs.

"GAV!"

If he killed someone because of me...

"No," I whispered. It was stupid of me to taunt him.

Stupid of me to tempt him to kill. And if he wouldn't kill me, he would kill someone.

"Gav—"

His name caught in my throat.

He was my entire world right now. And I was just a toy for him to play with. He never loved me. I didn't even know if he was capable of love. But the emotion inside of me swelled and swelled, and I couldn't get rid of it.

How could I love someone like that? What kind of horrible person would I have to be, to love a serial killer?

He was the angel of death, but he had brought me life again. He had shone a light onto the things that mattered. It was only after losing everything that I realized what was really important in life. And what was important to me?

Him, a small voice whispered. *Only him.*

He had played the game well. Trade by trade, I had given him the shattered pieces of me. And he had taken those pieces, put them back together. He had shown me a side of life that I had never seen.

Was it a game? I didn't know. I didn't care. Forget everything the rest of the world cared about. I didn't need to be beautiful, or wear pretty clothes. I didn't need to lose weight or go to parties. I didn't need to tally up friends one by one until I was popular. Here I was, naked and alone, and my mind was clearer than it had ever been before.

All I needed was myself.

"Good," I mumbled. "Because all you have right now is yourself, you idiot."

I left the door and curled up in the bed, hugging my knees to my chest. I couldn't think about it. Wouldn't think about it. Wouldn't think about him, how he might be out there right now, bringing someone back to carve them up...

No. Stop.

I lay there for hours, willing myself to shut off that part of my brain. I didn't have a panic attack, though. Whenever my anxiety threatened to bubble up, I tamped it back down, thinking about the way the tree branches had waved above our heads. Thinking about the newts I had seen, trying so desperately to get away.

My thoughts drifted back to him, over and over again. To the bruises I'd seen in the photographs. To the way he looked when he plunged inside of me, and then afterward. His eyes had sparked bright, and I thought that I might have saved him from that awful blankness that he called the shadow.

I blinked at the realization. It wasn't just myself that I cared about. I cared about him. I wanted to be his, to be the one to drive away the darkness inside of him.

I didn't realize that I had drifted off into sleep until the bolt outside the door snapped open and I raised my head. My cheeks were wet with tears. I was terrified to see what was on the other side of the door, but worse than that was not knowing.

The door swung open and he walked in, still holding the knife. His hair was mussed and there was a streak of dirt on the side of his face. His pants were dusty, cobwebs lacing his ankles.

But the knife—

The knife was clean. There was no blood on the

blade.

He sat down silently next to me on the bed, staring down at the knife in his lap.

"Where did you go?" I asked.

"The basement."

The basement? He had locked me up and terrified me, all for nothing?

"Why?" I asked, my heart beating fast.

"To see what it was like. I was curious."

"And?"

"It was dark."

He turned, raised his eyes to me. I saw emotion in there, a stark sadness that scared me.

"Gav?"

"Dress. Come with me."

He watched me quietly as I pulled on my clothes. Every glance of his felt like it bruised my skin. I wanted him to tie me up again. I wanted his arms around me. I wanted his touch. But he didn't touch me, not at all.

When I was dressed, he stood up and walked out of the room, the knife hanging loosely at his side. I followed him nervously. He had always had a hand on me before, and I wondered what he had decided to do with me.

Was he leading me to the kitchen? Was he going to hurt me? Had he decided, after all this, to kill me?

Before, he had put a hand on me to guide me. Now, he walked down the stairs. I paused at the statue before following him down the steps.

"Come on," he said, calling up to me. "Don't be afraid."

Those words chilled me. I came down the stairs

slowly and followed him across the living room, down the hallway to the front door. He opened the door.

"Go on," he said.

I stepped past him with my breath held. When I was in front of him, he could stab me from behind. He could slit my throat. He could—

"Kat."

I turned around to see him standing in the doorway, his knife hanging limply from one hand.

"Gavriel?"

"I'm sorry, kitten." His eyes were sad, so sad. It was all I could do not to run back to him, to take him in my arms, to comfort him. "Go on, now."

"What…" my voice trailed off as I realized that he wasn't following me out onto the porch. "What are you doing?"

"I'm letting you go."

The words buzzed around my ears, but I didn't comprehend what he was saying.

"For a walk?"

"Forever. You're free."

"Wh—Why?" I stammered. Every muscle in my body felt like it was made of lead. I stood on the porch, dumbfounded. I was still convinced that if I turned around, he would raise the knife, fling it forward into my back.

"You're right," he said, gesturing outside with an expansive wave of the knife. "This. All this. It doesn't matter. It's not real. I can't take your life away from you."

You've given me back my life, I wanted to say. *You've given me the only reason to live.* But my voice caught in my throat. Stupid, stupid. I should have turned to run before he could change his mind. Something told me that he wouldn't change his mind.

It's not real, he had said. What I had thought was something between us was nothing. And now he had pulled the rug out from under my feet. I had just accepted my fate, and now he was handing me another one. As ridiculous as it felt, I wanted nothing more than to run back inside, to stay with him.

"You're really letting me go?" I croaked.

"Yes. Stupid, I know. Maybe I am a stupid person, after all."

"That's not it." Why was I still there? Why was I not running away right now?

"It's because I'm bored, kitten," he said. His fingers tightened around the blade. "Bored with all of this. You have to go now."

He opened his mouth to say something else, then closed it. Stepping forward, he reached up and cupped my cheek in his hand. His palm was hot against my skin.

Don't do this, I cried inside. *Keep me. Want me. I need you to want me.*

But I said nothing.

He bent his head and brushed his lips against mine. The kiss was so light, and yet I felt electricity arc through my nerves at the barest touch.

I wanted him to stab me with the knife he held. I wanted to die in that moment, wanting something that I could never have. But he didn't raise the knife at all. I believe he had forgotten it was there.

"Goodbye, kitten."

"Goodbye."

He stepped back and closed the door behind him. I could hear the snap of the lock.

I stood on the porch for another moment, my body shaking, unsure what it was that had just happened. Then I turned and began to walk down the driveway, the sun shining brightly overhead.

CHAPTER TWENTY-SEVEN

Gav

The world closed in on me as the door swung shut behind her. Closed in - the walls disappeared into black. My body went numb.

She was gone.

Everything I'd worked to keep secret was out, the walls were broken. In my mind, I saw her running out to the road, sticking out her thumb. Catching a ride to the police station. They would come, they would knock down the door. What would they find?

As if underwater, I went to the bedroom. Pulled the arm chair around to the foot of the bed. Untied the rope from the bedposts.

The rope, useless. I would never tie her up again. Useless, useless, except for one thing. My hands moved automatically, looped the rope around itself. The knot tied itself, it seemed, and before I knew it the noose was finished, hanging limply from my hand.

Still in the bedroom, the rope slung over the high rafter, scraped the wood as I pulled it tight. Tied snug against the foot of the bed. The chair under my feet held steady, although my hands shook.

Me? I felt nothing. It wasn't me who took the noose and draped it around my neck. Not my hands which tightened the knot fast. The rope scratched the skin at my collarbone, but the sensation came from a distance, not from my own nerve endings. I was watching myself commit suicide.

Before, in the tub, I'd held the knife to my skin and recoiled. Now, though, there was nothing for me to recoil from. Just an empty room.

I took my last breath and stepped forward into nothing.

Kat

At the end of the driveway, I caught the motion sensor. The iron gate rattled open in front of me. I stared out at the curving road.

I didn't want to leave.

So ridiculous. Insane. But there was something at the back of my mind, something that was nagging at me. I didn't know what it was.

The sound of a car engine came to my ears as though from a distance. I could hear it coming around a lower bend in the road. All I had to do was run out into the middle of the road, wave my arms. I was free. I could go home.

What was it he had said that troubled me so much?

The car's engine grew louder, and I closed my eyes, my hands at my temples. Thinking back. He wanted to let me go. Surely he knew that I was going to go to the police. He hadn't even asked me not to tell anyone.

Bored.

The car came around the bend, but I was already running back up toward the house, the troubled feeling in my mind coalescing into something as clear and bright as words on a page. I knew what he meant.

Bored—that was the reason I'd tried to commit suicide. That was what I'd told him.

I ran up the porch and banged on the door, the feeling of dread growing inside of me.

"Gav!" I shouted. "Gav! Let me in!"

The door knob rattled in my hand, but the deadbolt was secure.

"Gav!"

No response.

I went to the window, banging on the pane. I tried to look in, but the glare of the sun reflected off of the glass, and I could see nothing inside. I raised my hand to break the windowpane, and then hesitated. But only for a second.

What is he going to do, kill me?

Gav

The darkness descended, but this time it was not the darkness of my shadow. Shadows need light to exist, and where I was going there was nothing, nothing at all.

Around my neck I felt a strange tug and tension cutting off my blood. My heart pounded loud, drowning out everything. My body kicked once, then again, and I only sensed the body kicking, could not feel it myself. I was already drifting away into the darkness.

This was a dark like fog, so thick it slid over my skin. A soft, enveloping darkness. A peaceful void that I fell into knowingly, longing to lose myself. It was the same thing you sink into halfway on your way to sleep - an ether, thick and palpable. The murmuring fog cradled me, turning me in its arms.

My breath stopped. My lungs were empty. I was empty, blissfully empty. The sound of my heartbeat faded, slowed to a dull murmur. The shadow of a heartbeat.

The sound of the fog - lord, how can I describe it? Pick up a shell and hold it to your ear. It's not the ocean you hear, but rather a reverberation of static noise. That was the sound of the fog, a low roar coming from nowhere and filling everything. It was a dull roar, a noise that tickled at my senses without letting me hear anything else. The sound came through my body and filled me, too, a peaceful static.

The noose tightened on my neck, but it didn't hurt. Nothing hurt. I was weightless now, floating away into the dark fog, leaving my shadow and all shadows behind.

Kat

I broke through the window, stepping carefully inside so I wouldn't cut myself.

"Gav!" I cried.

I checked the living room, the kitchen. He wasn't

there. I heard a noise from upstairs. The bedroom. I stumbled up the steps and raced down the hallway.

"Gav!"

I banged open the door and saw the rope, the chair, and his body, his beautiful body, hanging limp in the middle of the air. Like he was floating.

___Gav___

Perfect, this darkness. It was not the shadow at all. The shadow was gone, far away. All of my sins would be suffocated, drowned in the fog. I let myself drift, feeling calm. Peaceful.

Then, from away, far far in the distance, buried in the fog, I heard a scream.

___Kat___

My fingers fumbled at the knot, but it was too tight. His entire weight had pulled the knot, and I couldn't undo it. His face was white, and his lips were beginning to turn blue-grey, the same color as his eyes.

"No, no, no," I mumbled, casting my eyes around. There it was. The knife on the dresser. I grabbed it and swung the blade hard at the bedpost, cutting the rope right through the knot.

Gav

With a hard jolt, I was yanked back ungently into my body. All was dark, still, though my shadow had yet to reappear. There was still peace around me in this darkness. The tension around my neck loosened and gave way, but I clung to the dark fog.

A sharp pressure on my chest made me gasp, and I heard the blood in my body start to pump again. My pulse thudded in my ears.

A heartbeat. Sobbing. The peaceful fog began to recede. I clutched for it, and it slipped away uselessly through my fingers. _No! My chance to escape!_

From the place I had already left, her voice was calling.

"Don't go," she cried. Her words faded in and out like a poorly tuned radio, becoming clearer as the darkness receded. "Don't die. Oh god, don't die."

I wanted to tell her not to pray for me. God, if such a thing existed, wouldn't intervene to save the life of a killer. Then again, He might have a sense of humor.

Kat

His body crumpled to the ground, lifeless. I slid my fingers under the noose at his neck and pulled it over his head, throwing it to the side.

"_No_," I moaned. "No, please, no. Don't die."

He wasn't breathing. I pressed my fingers to his wrist, feeling for a pulse. My own heart was pounding so hard that I couldn't hear anything.

"Come on, Gav," I whispered. I bent down and pressed my lips against his. My breath lifted his chest, filled his lungs. My hands pressed down on his chest, hard and fast, desperate to draw the life back into him. Lips to his, I breathed again.

Again.

I couldn't lose him.

I couldn't.

Gav

Slowly at first, the fog seeped away, then faster, drawing all of the nothingness away with it. Taking away with it my peace. Her voice was louder, clearer, right in my ear. Her hands beat at my chest, her sobs audible.

"Come back. Don't leave me. *Please, Gavriel. Come back.*"

Clinging to the darkness, I felt her hand grasp at my fingers. I knew she was reaching for me. I could have tried to stay gone forever, but the ground was being pulled away from under my feet.

There was no fog anymore, only the darkness without peace, and I knew that this was not a place I could stay in. Somebody was calling.

I wasn't sure if I was doing the right thing, but when has that ever stopped me?

She reached for me, and I could not wait forever.

Scared, unsure, I took her hand and let her pull me back into the light.

CHAPTER TWENTY-EIGHT

*   Kat   *

With a gasp, his eyes opened. I fell back, sobbing, as his lungs drew in ragged gasps of air. His skin pinkened, the color coming back to his lips.

"Gav," I whispered, my hands holding his. The rope had left a mark around his neck, a deep red gouge. He coughed and rolled onto his side.

I waited for him to catch his breath. His fingers were splayed out on the floor, and I pulled back away from him. Now that he was back—

He was dangerous.

No.

He was a killer.

No.

What are you doing? Run. Run!

I shook the thoughts from my head. The muscles in my right arm ached, and I realized that I had strained myself when I swung the knife into the bedpost. I didn't care. Nothing mattered except that he was alive.

Gav pulled himself up, slouching against the bed. He closed his eyes, drawing in a deep breath, then exhaled. I waited, scared, sitting on the floor.

Finally he opened his eyes. His voice was scratchy, hollow. He could barely speak.

"Why did you come back?" he whispered.

My heart beat fast in my chest.

"I realized what you were doing. I knew you wouldn't let me go for any other reason. I figured out what you were going to do."

He smiled, the motion making him wince in pain. He rubbed his neck with one hand.

"Kitten, that doesn't answer my question. Why did you come back?"

The real answer slipped from my tongue before I could stop it.

"I love you."

He looked at me, his eyes softening.

"That's why I let you go," he whispered.

"Because…"

"Because I love you. It's a weakness, isn't it, kitten?"

He smiled. Oh, lord, he smiled.

I nodded slowly, my heart swelling in my chest.

"Yes. A good weakness."

His breath came back to him. He reached for the rope and took it up in his hand, turning it over and over.

"I was almost there," he murmured. "Almost dead."

The thought sent ice through my veins. Just thinking about his body hanging from the ceiling made me want to scream again.

"Did you see anything?" I asked.

"Nothing to see," he said, tossing the rope off to the side. "I suppose now we simply have to live."

We.

The word was a fingernail plucking my nerves. Vibrating them. He coughed again.

"What happens now, kitten? Have you thought that

far?"

I hadn't thought that far, but apparently my subconscious had started to. The pieces clicked into place one by one as I thought about it.

I moved over to where he was sitting against the bed and sat with him, shoulder to shoulder. The explanation came to my lips mechanically. I ticked off the points one after another.

"I tell everyone I had a panic attack. I ran away to be alone for a while with my friend."

"A friend?"

"A secret friend, one I'd never told anybody about. You get away scot-free. And…"

"Yes?"

"And you pay for me to go back to school in the fall."

"Oh?" His eyebrow raised.

"It's a fair trade."

"A trade? What do I get in return?"

I paused. There was no hesitation in my heart, but I didn't know how he would take it. His head turned to the side, and he stared into my eyes.

"Me." My hands pressed into the floor, holding me still. "All of me."

"All of you."

His hand lifted. His knuckles grazed my elbow. He moved his hand down, brushing his fingertips along my arm.

"You would be mine?"

"Yes." My voice was shaky. After all this, his rejection would be the thing that would hurt me the most. His hand glided down my lower arm and his fingers slipped loosely around my wrist. I could feel his thumb pressing against my pulse point. Where my scar was.

"You've spent a lot of time and effort trying *not* to be mine, kitten."

"I—I didn't know what I wanted before."

"And now?"

"I want you. And I want to be yours."

His hand tightened around my wrist and he lifted my hand to his mouth.

His lips kissed my palm at the heel. I didn't breathe. Couldn't breathe. I was balancing on the edge of something dangerous, I knew. But I didn't care. All I wanted was to be his.

Finally he spoke, the whisper tickling my skin.

"Yes. That sounds nice, kitten."

Gav

I pulled her to me, then. She, who had seen the shadow inside of me. She, who had been trapped for so long in my home, She had left… and come back.

She had saved me.

There was no trace of the shadow as I lifted her in my arms, lay her down on the bed. There was no trace of it when I kissed her hard, so hard that I lost my own breath in the whirlwind of passion. Hands, clothes flew everywhere.

I needed her so badly. Needed to know—

"It's really you, isn't it?" I asked, my hand splayed across her cheek. Dark soulful brown eyes gazed up at me.

"Of course."

"This isn't a hallucination? A dream? I'm not dead?"

"If you were dead, what would this be?" she asked, reaching down and grabbing my hip, pulling me against her body with a groan of desire that sent light exploding in my mind.

"Heaven," I whispered.

"You really think you died and went to heaven?" She smirked, and the strangest thing happened. A bubbling inside that turned into laughter, pure laughter. I fell against her body, laughing uncontrollably. At last I wiped the tears from my eyes.

"Good point. I concede the argument."

Her fingers were touching me now, pulling at my length. Already aroused, I growled in her ear and flipped her back, pinning her wrists back to the bed. She grinned at me and twisted, sending new flames of lust through my body as her soft curves moved under me.

"Do I need to tie you up?" I teased.

"Please," she whispered. Her lips were plump and pink, so innocent and yet so demanding. I kissed her again, kissed her and kissed her and could not stop until she gasped for breath. Then I got the rope.

I paused after finishing the last knot. Her body was stretched across the bed, ready and willing. The rose-red slit between her legs was hot and swollen. I ran a single finger down her thigh, tracing the outline of her mound, wetting myself with her juices. I tasted her sweetness and she moaned. I could see her hips jerking upward slightly, wanting me to take her.

"Gavriel—"

I paused then. I looked around the room. Everything was the same. The sunlight came through the window the same as it always had. The bed was in the same place. And yet, there was no hint of the shadow.

She had driven it away.

Her chestnut eyes watched my every move as I climbed into bed and positioned myself between her legs. I loved the little jerks of her body, the twisting muscles in her arms as she strained against the ties. I could have watched her forever.

"Gav?"

My mind came back to the present. I leaned down, my cock sliding against the deliciously slick opening. She gasped as I found her slit and entered, letting her folds caress my tip. Then I thrust hard, stabbing her with my whole self, plunging deep into oblivion.

When I spoke in her ear, my breath was already ragged.

"Thank you," I said. "Thank you for saving me."

Kat

He teased me. He tortured me.

Most of all, he satisfied me. Satisfied my every single urge in ways I couldn't have imagined before him. His hands spanked my skin raw and red and I begged him for more. His cock filled me, pushing me to the outer edge of my limits, and my screams were screams of delight. He twisted my nipples, sucked bruises on my hip, licked my wrists until I came from only his tongue touching me in places I'd never known I wanted to be touched.

He rolled himself against me, swollen rock hard and throbbing, and I matched his rhythm and he made me come against his cock, my body milking him, clenched viselike and shivering. He pulled out and made me come again with his tongue.

And when I ached too much, when every part of me was shattered and wide open, he pressed his thumb against my lips and I sucked hard, licked the pad of his brilliant fingers. Without waiting for a breath, he split me open with his thickness and pressed a finger between my ass cheeks and filled me in every hole, and climax after climax shuddered my body, leaving me empty of anything except the desire for more, more—

For hours he took me, used me, and gave me back myself.

When he was done at last, my breath was jagged in the air. My eyes were closed and I only felt his fingers at the ropes around my wrists. The knots loosened and opened and then he was rubbing my wrists with his hands, massaging them deeply.

I opened my eyes and saw him examining my wrists, the red lines from the rope standing out brightly on my skin.

"Would you like to get rid of them?" he asked softly.

"What?"

"The scars. Do you want the surgery? We could clean them up for you."

"We?"

"I have an old friend. He's a cosmetic surgeon."

I looked down at the white seams on the insides of my wrists. They caught the light and gleamed, just for a moment, shining brightly. Like my soul was peeking through the thin parts of me.

"You would be there?"

"I would assist."

I raised my eyebrows as he lay down beside me. His hand cupped my breast and he nuzzled into the side of me. I had never thought about getting rid of my scars. Even in the summer, I would wear long sleeves to hide them. To be able to walk around freely, without worrying… it was tempting.

"You would assist, because…"

"For one, there's nobody else I would trust to come into my home."

"Oh! You would do it here?"

"Yes."

"Where?"

"You know where, kitten."

I thought of the kitchen table, the straps. The blood. *The man he had murdered. He was a murderer.*

My inner self was more intelligent than my outer body, and I squirmed uncomfortably, thinking about the idea.

"You wouldn't be tied," he said. "You would be drugged. Local anesthesia."

"I wouldn't be zonked out?"

"No."

"But this friend of yours, then, he would know about us? About you?"

He blinked deliberately. Stalling. There could only be one reason for his hesitation.

"He already knows?"

"He's… he's like me. In certain ways. In others, not so much."

"How so?"

"He's much less patient than I am."

I stared at the man who had tied me up and teased me to the edge of insane desire. Someone worse than him?

"You're skirting the question, kitten," he said.

"I…"

I looked down at the lines once more. I closed my eyes and tried to imagine them gone. Tried to imagine my skin bare and unpuckered again. The image in my mind was of myself, but younger. Fifteen. Before I had taken a knife to my veins.

"No." The word left my mouth as if of its own accord.

"No? You don't want them removed?"

"No."

"Why not?"

I turned my face up toward him. I thought of the box inside his closet. All those pictures of him as a boy, covered in bruises.

"Why do you keep those photographs?"

His jaw clenched, sending the vein at his temple pulsing. He took a deep breath and relaxed.

"I shouldn't. I shouldn't remember the pain."

"But you'll feel the pain of the past no matter

what," I said. "And remembering this way… it shows you the danger inside of you."

"It reminds you how dangerous you are?" He smiled. "How dangerous are you, kitten?"

"I'm more dangerous than you. Suicide is the ultimate escape route."

"Is that what it was? Escape?"

"Maybe."

He paused, looking down at the scars on my wrists.

"I wished that I could escape," he said. "I wished it every night when I heard her crying. I wished it every night when he came up to my room. And one night, when he swung the door open, his belt already half-undone, I wished that he would go away.

"I wished that he would go hurt *her*."

"Gav—" I wanted to stop him from telling me this. This was a confession that I could not comprehend. As bad as my parents had been, it had never been that bad.

"I wanted him to stop hitting me and hurt her instead. And he did. He hurt her so bad that I did something I never did. She screamed and screamed and finally I couldn't take it. I ran downstairs and into their room, something I was *never* allowed to do. Not under any circumstances, understand? And there he was, with the knife. And there she was, the blood soaking into the carpet like a dark wine stain. She was still beautiful."

His shoulders shuddered. His mouth twitched.

"Still as beautiful as the day."

"You don't know what happened to him? Your father? You don't know where he is?"

"No. If I did know, I would be there right now with a syringe in one hand and a father's day card in the other." His mouth quirked. "I'm a terrible son."

"You've never had a chance."

"Maybe. Maybe I should have killed him before he killed her."

His eyelids fluttered at that, cast down.

"So you don't want to remove your scars?" he asked again, quietly.

"No." I was firmer now. Resolved.

"Why? Because you might forget? Is that the only reason?"

"No. It's…" I closed my eyes, trying to make the right words form in my mind. "It's because they remind me of how close I came to never being here right now."

"And where are you right now?" he murmured.

I cradled his head against my chest. His arms wrapped around me, his palms warm against my lower back. His ear was pressed against me like he wanted to sink into my flesh.

"I'm here," I said simply. "I'm here with you."

The End

Thank you for reading HIS

If you enjoyed the story would you please consider leaving a review on your favorite retailer?

Just a few words and some stars really does help!

Also, be sure to sign up for my mailing list to find out about new releases, deals and giveaways!

http://bit.ly/ADarkNewsletter